THE
CHANGELING
OF
FENLEN
FOREST

Katherine Magyarody

yellow dog

Yellow Dog
(an imprint of Great Plains Publications)
1173 Wolseley Avenue
Winnipeg, MB R3G 1H1
www.greatplains.mb.ca

Great Plains Publications gratefully acknowledges the financial support provided for its publishing program by the Government of Canada through the Canada Book Fund; the Canada Council for the Arts; the Province of Manitoba through the Book Publishing Tax Credit and the Book Publisher Marketing Assistance Program; and the Manitoba Arts Council.

Design & Typography by Relish New Brand Experience
Printed in Canada by Friesens

Library and Archives Canada Cataloguing in Publication

Title: The changeling of Fenlen Forest / Katherine Magyarody.
Names: Magyarody, Katherine, author.
Identifiers: Canadiana (print) 20190056282 | Canadiana (ebook) 20190056290 |
  ISBN 9781773370194 (softcover) | ISBN 9781773370200 (EPUB) |
  ISBN 9781773370217 (Kindle)
Classification: LCC PS8626.A37575 C53 2019 | DDC jC813/.6—dc23

ENVIRONMENTAL BENEFITS STATEMENT

Great Plains Publications saved the following resources by printing the pages of this book on chlorine free paper made with 100% post-consumer waste.

TREES	WATER	ENERGY	SOLID WASTE	GREENHOUSE GASES
5	430	2	18	2,330
FULLY GROWN	GALLONS	MILLION BTUs	POUNDS	POUNDS

Environmental impact estimates were made using the Environmental Paper Network Paper Calculator 4.0. For more information visit www.papercalculator.org.

Canada

FSC
www.fsc.org
MIX
Paper from responsible sources
FSC® C016245

CHAPTER ONE

Missing

Ma raised me alone under the reaching shadows of Old Fenlen Forest, at the end of the civilized world. It was her and me in our small log house, and the mule trying to sneak into our vegetable patch.

We weren't always alone. When I was very small, my smiling, whistling father was with us. The three of us rode in a pony cart and we sold horn spoons and copper pots and spools of ribbons and fine-toothed combs and beauty ointments all down the old stone roads that start at Gersa's capital of Terth and fan out like a star. Our fortune was made on the lesser cart tracks that connect the high roads like the uneven lines of a spider's web.

Pa told us that west was best because he loved riding into the sunset. But one day, we changed directions and started riding east, squinting, towards the rising dawn. The old roads brought us through all the towns, villages and hamlets in East Gersa, until tall grass started forcing itself between the paving stones that tumbled into the ditches. A day after the last village, the gently sloping road petered out at the edge of the forest.

There were no more people we could sell to in this direction, but my father said we couldn't go back up the road. I no longer remember what reason he gave. But the next morning the dusty grey pony was gone, and my father with it. Ma and I waited for him to come back, to hitch up the pony again and take us in a new direction. After three days, our food ran out. We never kept sacks of flour and oats or loops of sausage like people do in houses because we were used to trading for our food. But you cannot eat ribbons and combs, and we had already eaten the beauty ointment, which was only honey, rough sugar and herbs, after all.

Ma put herself in the harness of the pony cart and heaved as if her heart were breaking, but she could not get the wheels to turn. She picked me up, but she was too weak to carry me back up the hill. I was still too young to walk so far at night. She put me in the small trundle bed and turned up our blanket, a rough weave of old fabric ends that we had never been able to sell. She set a skin of water beside me.

"You stay here," she said. "And if your father comes back, he will find me at the village. Tell him I am not afraid." She pressed her dry lips to my forehead and was gone into the evening shadows.

If you have ever been alone, you will know that time stretches into infinity and your thoughts loom over you. If I had been older, I would have tried to sleep by imagining myself into a better place. But I was too young to think of anything other than the truth. I was alone for the first time. My mother had left me, and I was sure that I would be eaten by bears long before my father came back.

Come, Pa, come, I prayed.

If you have ever been alone, you know that sounds become louder and the hairs rise up along your body, waiting for some sign of a predator. I was sick with fear at each creak of wind pushing through the wood of the pony cart, each rasp of wool and silk and samite as I pulled the blanket closer around myself. My own heartbeat was deafening.

Come, Pa, come.

And then there was a gust that shook the little pony cart and made the metal traces sing. I heard something outside, the slow, deliberate alternations of weight from hoof to hoof. It was him. He would swoop me up, hug me close and feed me sugared plums. Hope made me strong, and I pulled myself from the bed and ran to the door draped in my piebald blanket. I swung the little door open and saw...darkness. He would be on the other side of the cart, giving the pony a rub-down. I kicked down the wooden stairs and ran to the other side, spreading my arms to catch him.

Darkness.

The weak sliver of the moon barely shone off the creek, the meadow grass, the looming trees.

But I had heard right. There, there it was—a gleam, a smear of dark grey against the black silhouette of the massive forest.

"Wait!" I screamed. He thought we had abandoned him. Heartbroken, he was leaving. I ran as fast as I could towards the grey and, as I approached, the shape swung out of the shadows toward me. I froze. It was not my father. It was not a bear. It was something much more terrifying.

Sixteen hands at the muscular, scarred shoulder. A lank mane and tail the colour of ghost's tears and tangled with dead leaves. A heavy head tilted down in suspicion. And the long, spiralling horn that ended in a delicate, rounded point mere inches from my heart.

I closed my eyes. A tear squeezed out between my eyelids and began to slide down my cheek towards my mouth. I imagined that the salt taste would be the last thing I sensed.

Instead, something smooth and cool touched my cheek. When I opened my eyes, the unicorn was lifting her horn away and feeling my tear trickle down the groove of the ivory. She—though I did not know she was a doe at the time—tilted her head to the side and considered me with a solemn, dark blue gaze. I stared back. People think that unicorns are the colour of bridal satin, of pearls, of fresh milk. A unicorn that colour wouldn't have five minutes' peace with all the poachers after them. My doe-unicorn was a dull, dappled silver that shimmered only dimly in the moonlight. I think I was able to see her only because I desperately *needed* to see something in the dark. That is the poachers' mistake. They only *want* to see their unicorns and are happy enough to go home with a rabbit or a red deer slung behind them. There is no man-made trick of finding them, only a need, though I did not know it then.

My unicorn made a sound that would have been a nicker coming from a horse. She stepped forward. I felt her hot breath on my face as she passed her velvet lips along my hair and nudged me towards her chest with her chin. She smelled like the freshly churned mud from her cloven hooves, like newly unfurled leaves, like acacia honey. I put my hand gently on her muscular shoulder and felt the crisscrossing of scars. The hair was longer and downier than that of our pony, softer to the touch. The unicorn turned slowly. Keeping my hand in place, I turned with her.

I was at peace that night. I don't remember much else. I think I saw the unicorn shake fruit from the trees using her horn; this memory comes vividly whenever I encounter the sour taste of wild plums. However, I do remember waking up to the slow thud-thud of my doe-unicorn's heartbeat and opening my eyes to see the shifting green-gold canopy of aspen leaves at the edge of the forest. I remember Ma arriving on horseback with a man and a woman, remember her seeing the open, abandoned pony cart and her running toward it, calling my name in a hoarse scream. She collapsed on the stairs. She sank her fingers into her thick, dark hair and began to pull. The two villagers dismounted and ran to stop her from hurting herself, but they both stopped short when they saw me and my doe-unicorn walking towards them.

I had been watching all of this as we took our measured

steps together. I was too young to understand; I felt certain that the miracle of the unicorn, that the sight of us together, would stun the grief from my mother. When she looked up, the harsh creases at the edges of her mouth relaxed slightly. Her fingers eased from her hair. But Ma did not smile. Not like the others. They were struck by the sight of the unicorn, but she was my mother first and the witness of a miracle second.

The man had a spear with him, in case of boars or bears, but when he saw my unicorn, he let it fall. The plump, grey-haired woman covered her mouth with her hand, but even so, I could see the happy curves of her mouth. The unicorn nudged me towards my mother and I went. She waited patiently until Ma's arms were around me. The villagers' eyes turned towards us and when we all looked up again, the unicorn was gone.

Though we did not know it yet, the forest had already claimed me as its own.

Ma pulled me up in front of her in the saddle and we rode to the village, where we stopped at a large, comfortable house with black beams that stood out securely from the pale wattle and daub. Before she handed me to the man, Ma whispered that the two villagers with us were the headman, Nicholas Helder, and his mother and that I was to behave. As I was deposited in the hands of the headman, it became obvious that he was unused to holding children. He let all my weight lie in the hard curve between his thumbs and his forefingers. Instead of bringing me easily to his chest, as my father would have done, he set me down at arm's length. "You gave us a right scare," he said, as if being left alone in the pony cart had been my idea.

But Mrs. Helder winked at me and took my hand. She asked me if I wanted apricot jam or apple butter on my scones.

My mother and I sat down at a wide-planked table. As Mrs. Helder brought out crocks of jam and unlocked the scones from the tin breadbox, Nicholas Helder collected a quill, ink, paper and a sand-shaker. "Well," he said as he sat down, "now you've got your child, where will you go?"

"As long as there is a chance my husband will come back for us, it's best if we stay," Ma said. "Perhaps I could sell my stock at the village?"

Nicholas Helder's beard rasped against the collar of his shirt as he shook his head. "With all respect to you, lady, they've had enough of thin-bottomed pots and frayed ribbons." He laid out the sheets of paper. "I cannot force them to buy what they do not want."

"Then we have nothing."

"Do you have money to buy another pony? Can you carry on the trade elsewhere?"

"The money is gone."

"Do you have anywhere to go?" Nicholas Helder said.

"No."

Nicholas Helder and his mother exchanged a glance.

"Any family that can take you in?" asked Mrs. Helder gently, as she spread apricot jam on my scone.

Ma pursed her lips. "My husband never had any."

There was a long pause. I tried to chew quietly. Were they trying to send us away?

"Can't we stay?" I said. "What if Pa comes back?"

Again, that quick glance between the two of them.

"Well, there's that," Mrs. Helder said, as she buttered my second scone. "And if...well, there *is* the fact of the unicorn."

I saw my chance to press my case. "It's my friend," I said. "It can help me find Pa."

"Strange things happen in the Fenlen Forest," said Nicholas quickly. "That's why it's never been logged. You could stay with us until you get sorted. You'll be hired easy for the harvest. Even the little girl."

"After selling them, what was it? Thin-bottomed pots and frayed ribbons? We'd need something better to offer."

"Why not," Mrs. Helder said into the silence that followed my mother's stiff declaration. "Why not listen to the child? The unicorn has chosen her. That must mean something. Go out and see if it will come back. Sometimes the hunters find old horns at the forest's edge. What do they call it? Alicorn?"

"Yes. That's the apothecary's name for unicorn horn," Ma said swiftly. Her brows were tensed. Curiosity was beginning to crowd out sadness and anger. My heart leapt, for I did not like when she was sharp.

"Right," said Mrs. Helder. "Alicorn. If your little girl found one, it would set you right up. You know what the alicorn is worth." She paused, but no one answered. "It protects against sickness," she insisted, "against poison. Ground up, you could use it as a restorative. As a beautifier. No more fake ointments that housewives could cook up themselves. The real thing."

"Yes!" I said, seeing my chance to please Ma and find my unicorn again, before Pa came back for us. "I could find it!"

"This isn't the time for fairy stories, Mam." Nicholas Helder cleared his throat. "Mayhap the man will turn up in a day or two, and the family can be on its merry way. All right, then," he picked up his quill and dipped it in the ink. "Now tell me, my lady…"

"Sylvia. That's my name," Ma said sharply, warding off any trace of sarcasm.

"Sylvia, tell me what your man looks like. There's a press at Wealdton. I can have a broadsheet printed up and sent to the larger towns."

Ma described my father and Nicholas Helder leaned over the table, scratching away with a quill. As I watched him making broad marks across the paper, I got up with my third scone in hand and sidled over.

"What does that say?" I asked, pointing at the first and largest words.

"Tinker, Missing."

"That's his name." I always heard men call my father Tinker.

"And what's yours? Is it Curly?" He tousled my messy brown hair.

"Elizabeth Missing."

He gave a strange smile. "You mean Elizabeth Tinker?"

"No," my mother said, from where she had been staring into the fire. "Not Tinker. Not any longer."

Nicholas Helder shook sand over the sheet of paper to soak up the excess ink. Ma watched him and ran one meditative finger over the wooden grooves of the table.

"If you are finished, may I write a letter?"

He gaped at her—that he could write was rarity enough, let alone a tinker's abandoned wife. "Then you *do* have family who might help you?"

"I do not know," Ma said. "We shall see."

By nightfall, Ma was Lady Missing to the village men because of her clear accent, neat features, and her strange ability to write. She was Poor Sylvia Missing to the women, who whispered that they pitied her and who attributed her stiffness to a rumour that she had been high born. But I am getting ahead of myself.

CHAPTER TWO

Visitors

The next day, the Helders drove us back to the pony cart in a small wagon loaded with a bushel of apples and root vegetables, a ham, a wheel of cheese, a sack of oats, and two nanny goats for milk. They also loaned us a bundle of gardening implements and a pouch of seeds. If we were staying for any amount of time, Mrs. Helder reckoned, we might as well grow some winter cabbage, turnips, beets, and radishes.

When we arrived at the pony cart, Nicholas Helder went with Ma to check for any repairs that might be needed. Meanwhile, Mrs. Helder fussed over me. She combed and braided my wild hair and fed me slices of apple.

My father used to cut me slices of apple, but first he used to peel it in a long, unbroken, scarlet spiral. "Do you think Pa will come back?"

"I can't say," she said slowly. "Elizabeth, whether your Ma decides that you should stay or go, you should know some of the stories told about Old Fenlen Forest. There is a reason why only the hungriest men hunt here. There is a reason why Gersa ends here. Do you know what lies beyond Gersa in that forest?"

"Philistion?" It was the only other country I had ever heard of.

She shook her head. "No. Even if Philistion looks like it belongs on the north-east side of the forest on a map, some people say that if you walked across that forest in a straight line, you would never arrive. The forest paths are said to twist and change and disappear. No…beyond Fenlen, there is another world where strange and wonderful things belong."

"Like unicorns?"

"Like unicorns," Mrs. Helder assured me. "And the Old Folk. They are said to pass through here sometimes. Some people say they're ghosts, or the spirits of lost hunters. Some people say they steal children who run away from home." She tapped me on the nose to break the spell. "I know *I* would steal you away in a minute, if I were Old Folk," she added with a wink.

"If Old Folk found me, could they take me to Pa?" Having seen a unicorn only yesterday, I trusted everything Mrs. Helder told me.

But Mrs. Helder shook her head. "No, child. There are legends of people wandering into that forest to catch a rabbit and never coming back. Or coming out to find that their grandchildren were old men and women…and they had not aged a bit. No, Elizabeth. Go with a unicorn if you must, but stay away from strangers."

"What stories are you telling her, Mam? Weren't the goats enough folly for one day?" Nicholas Helder had returned and was letting the goats off the back of the wagon. Mrs. Helder gave him a look as he passed a wheel of cheese to my mother.

"Stories have no price," Mrs. Helder said. "If that's what you mean by folly."

"In time, we will pay you for the goats thrice over," Ma said in a voice that made Nicholas Helder turn red.

"You have faith in your daughter's gift," Mrs. Helder said, giving me an affectionate pat on the cheek.

"Perhaps."

All through the day, I waited for my unicorn to come. But the unicorns were not our first visitors.

They arrived a few weeks later—though by then, I felt as though we had lived by the forest's edge for all eternity. Ma was cooking up porridge—again—and I was picking firewood. I had just stood up with my arms full of dry branches, when I thought I saw my unicorn watching me from between two aspen trees. I blinked, and when I opened my eyes again, there was no unicorn at all, just another tree, a bit in the distance. I had been hoping just a little too hard.

"Elizabeth! Come quickly!"

The fire must be dying down. I raced out of the forest and around the pony cart to where my mother held a wooden spoon suspended in the cooking pot. Under the pot, the coals were still glowing hot, and behind Ma, there was a good stack of firewood.

"Ma?"

Ma did not say anything to me. She was turned away from the forest. Through a veil of smoke, she watched the slope that lead to the village. I followed her gaze.

Two strangers were riding down the hill.

A man and boy sat astride matching, broad-necked palominos with coats of wheat gold and glossy white manes. In contrast to his horse's colour, the man wore a coat of fine black wool. His coat was buttoned tight to the waist with many small braid buttons, then flowed loose to the tops of his riding boots. Around his waist, he wore a scarlet silk sash that matched his broad-cuffed gloves. He wore a sword and dagger, both simply wrought but elegant. He must have been sweating in the hot early-autumn afternoon, but a broad-brimmed hat cast shade over his face. The other, a boy of about thirteen, wore a similar coat of sky blue and his boots were buttery suede. A bow was slung over the horn of his saddle. A quiver of arrows slapped between his shoulder blades in time with his horse's gait.

"Are those hunters?" I asked Ma. "Are they here for the unicorns?"

My questions seemed to snap Ma out of her reverie. She rounded on me.

"Oh, Elizabeth! *What* are you wearing?"

I looked down at myself. As usual, I was in a knee-length shift, same as any grubby child. Ma took three steps over, spat on the edge of her apron and tried to rub some dirt from my face. "And your hair!" She had braided it this morning, but much of it had escaped and corkscrewed around my face like the rays of a small, dark sun. She ran her fingers over my head and then held my hand tight. "It can't be helped now," she said.

"Gods strike me blind! Is that you, Sylvia?" The man's voice was deep and sonorous, like he was used to talking in big rooms, in front of crowds. The horses halted ten paces away from us.

"And is that you, Victor?" Ma answered in a fair imitation of the man. She stepped forward, dragging me alongside her. "You should have sent word that you were coming. I have not had time to prepare for your arrival." We were now quite close to the horses, whom I liked, but not as much as my unicorn.

"Well, I wanted to see—in full honesty—what would drive my dear sister to ask for my help."

Sister? I peered up at the man, Victor. He had a close-clipped, black beard and his face was the waxy yellow of a candle, like he was unused to being outside. The boy beside him, on the other hand, was a healthy brown. They both shared my mother's straight nose and firm jaw. Like her, they had a natural, hawk-like haughtiness. I had never thought of my mother as belonging to anyone but me and Pa.

Ma tightened her grip on my hand and raised her chin. "Well, how do you find me?"

"Hmmm." Victor dismounted, dropped his reins and stepped

towards her. Ma put out her other hand. He took it, stepped close and kissed her cheek. "Better than expected."

The boy piped up. "Grandmother said we mustn't hope. That we must expect you'd have lost all your teeth and your looks, and we'd find you soused in a jug of sour ale." He launched himself from the saddle and, taking both sets of reins, tied the horses to one of the pony cart's harness poles.

They were staying, then? I looked up at Ma, but she was smiling thinly at the boy.

"How kind. And you must be…?"

"Julian."

"Marina's boy," Victor supplied. "Your nephew."

"Ah, the little heir of the estate? You've grown since I saw you last."

The boy shrugged and sauntered around our campsite as if he owned it. "I'm hungry. Can we eat?" Julian peered over the edge of the pot and wrinkled his nose. "Never mind." He went over to his horse and pulled off his gloves. I saw the glitter of gold rings as he scrounged some dried apricots from his saddlebag. They looked like old-person's ears, but I wanted one very much. I wriggled my hand out of my mother's grip and trotted over.

Taking in my eager face, Julian extended his hand and dangled a dried apricot above me. I reached for it, and he lifted his arm higher. I jumped, and he threw the apricot away from us. He laughed as I raced to catch the orange-pink treat, but it fell into the grass. As I groused for it, I listened to Ma and her brother.

"I *am* surprised to see you looking so well," Victor said, though he sounded almost bored. "Here's the short of it. You look well enough. You're still of breeding age…"

"Breeding age?" Ma hissed, yet Victor went on.

"So, we decided we could take you back, thought you could help take care of Mother with me." He hesitated. "And the estate, too, should you prove yourself worthy."

"If I helped manage the estate, would I get my alchemy room back?"

"Ah, the famous alchemy room that Father so objected to. I don't particularly care. Yes. The point is, we might still make a fine match for you. We could pretend the last eight years never happened. You've been at a convent or something."

"And how does Elizabeth fit into this story about the convent?"

"Who?" But I had looked up at my name and he caught my eye. He smiled uneasily and turned away.

"Well, she doesn't. Between Marina and me, we have enough heirs, so there's no need to acknowledge her."

"Acknowledge...How *dare* you?"

"Well, look at her." Victor looked unruffled. "She doesn't look like she belongs to us at all. She could muck along with the peasants her entire life and be satisfied."

They considered me, gnawing on a dried apricot with my dirty hands. It was like eating sunshine and leather at the same time.

"The mark of a good parent," Victor said, "is the character of the child."

Julian was walking towards me, tossing another dried apricot up and down in his hand. "Want another?" he said with a grin.

"Yes, please," I said, eager to show that Ma was a good parent. He held it out, and as I approached, he drew his arm back swiftly. This time, I was ready for the trick. But now he threw fast and hard, and the apricot whipped past the leaves of the first row of trees, into the forest.

"Manners, Julian!" I heard Victor chide, but I was running after the treat. After endless oatmeal, I would do anything for something so long-lasting and tasty as a dried apricot. I might even save part of it for later.

As I ran, I could hear my mother shouting. Not at me, but at Victor, or Julian, or perhaps both of them. But once I passed through the trees, the sound of her voice disappeared. Instead, I heard the purr of the breeze through the leaves and the whirr of insects rubbing their wings together. As I crouched down in the bushes, I decided that I liked the forest sounds better than people sounds. I wasn't sure I liked Julian, but I was glad he'd given me a way to escape.

But where was the apricot? It must be near here. I crawled forward on my hands and knees, running my hands over the dried leaves and grass. I must have gone too far. I stood up and turned, but instead of seeing the edge of the forest with the blue sky above and our pony cart in the meadow, all I saw was more trees.

CHAPTER THREE

Strange Folk

If I had been older, I would have been scared. Instead, I was strangely impressed with myself, that I had crawled so far and so fast without noticing. I would have started looking for the clearing, but just then, there was a rush of silver and a unicorn galloped past me at full speed.

A moment later, a slender tree trunk a bit ahead of me shattered. The tree crashed over, and the fallen canopy of leaves shivered into stillness.

How could a tree *shatter*? I walked forward quickly. Splinters of fresh, white wood surrounded the base of the trunk like a sunburst. Near the core of the tree, where its strength had lain, lodged a metal ball, the size of a goat's eye. I reached out and felt faint heat radiating from it. Before I could touch the ball, I heard the scuffle of leaves and a full-throated, masculine yell.

Victor or Julian?

I crouched down behind the stump. A young man, a hunter, ran up to where I had been standing moments before. The shredded tree behind which I cowered wasn't wide enough to shield me entirely, but even so, I was safe for a short time. He gazed around wildly for the unicorn, his eyes well above where I hid. In his hands was a long metal pipe that ended in a wooden handle. He pointed it around like I had seen men aiming crossbows. "How did I miss?" he muttered to himself. "I had her right in my sights. I never miss."

With a curse, he set the pipe-thing against the tree and took out a great hunting knife, with which he prised the metal ball from the tree. I watched the strange man, too frightened to move. His jacket and pantaloons were made of ragged, wine-dark velvet, worn patchy and streaked with mud. The fine linen shirt at the gaping throat of his jacket was yellowed with sweat, yet had an edging of fine lace. The thick rings on his grimy fingers were gold. His dark hair and beard had once been carefully tended, but now were growing overlong. As he took some grey-black powder from a horn case and rammed it and the metal ball down the pipe, the expression on the young hunter's burnished, straight-nosed face was proud and angry.

Though I was scared for the unicorn, I was more frightened for myself. I prayed he would jog off without ever seeing me, but I had no luck. A bit of the powder drifted down, and the strange, acrid smell made me sneeze.

He looked down. "Elizabeth?"

I gave a gasp and crouched lower to the ground. I had never seen this man before, yet he seemed familiar, somehow. Worse, the sneer curling his lips looked anything but friendly. The hunter contemplated his weapons, the killing-tube in his hands and the knife at his waist. He settled for leaning over me, fists on his hips.

"You nasty little cat. Do you know how long I've been in here, because of you?"

I shook my head. He was mad, I was frightened, and so this was a time to get away. I shifted the weight on my hands and knees so I could shuffle a little backwards.

"Oh, no you don't." One hand shot out and grabbed me by the hair. I whimpered and brought my hands up, hoping to sink my nails into his wrist.

"You're the one who finds unicorns, and now you're going to find one for me."

"I'm not! I won't!" What was he talking about? Had the

Helders gossiped? It had only been that one time! "Let me go!" My scratching didn't seem to bother him. I needed to find another way to free myself.

"Don't lie." He gave me a little shake. "Well, now you're going to help me make my fortune and get me out of this damned forest."

Instead I kicked him, hard, on the inside of his knee. In his surprise, his grip loosened and I scrambled away. A few seconds and he would be coming after me, and he was so much bigger than I was.

"Elizabeth! Get back here!"

There was a giant boulder ahead, fringed by massive cedar trees. I dodged behind it.

My scar-shouldered unicorn stood there, patiently breathing in the fresh, spicy smell of the cedars. Was *she* the unicorn I had seen bolt past me? She gave a jerk of her chin at a pile of smaller boulders, as if inviting me to come climb onto her. As I slung my leg over her back, I ran my hand up from her scarred shoulder to her withers. My racing heart slowed a little. Cautiously, the doe-unicorn stepped out from the screen of the trees.

"Look out!"

The young hunter was waiting, but even so, my unicorn was faster than he. She struck out with her forelegs, and he dropped his weapon before he could fire.

I dug my hands into the unicorn's mane as she galloped off. Looking over my shoulder, I saw the young hunter running after us, calling my name. I closed my eyes and pressed into the unicorn's down. His calling cut off abruptly, and the air grew cool, then chilly.

When I opened my eyes, I thought for a heart-stopping instant that I had fallen into a dream. Somehow, all around us, the branches on the trees were bare and skeletal. Like we had raced from the heat of harvest time into the bitterness of early winter.

The unicorn stopped, and at the unexpected change of pace, I slid sideways off her back, pulling out a handful of white-silver hair from her mane as I tumbled into a carpet of leaves that crackled with frost.

· I landed hard on my seat. Tears started from my eyes at the sudden, hard end to our flight. The doe-unicorn snuffled at my hair in apology.

As I tried to stop my tears by rubbing the heel of my hands into my eyes, I heard shrill, panicked bleating and a girl's murmured, lilting singing in a language I had never heard.

I looked up and scrambled to my feet. Working in our garden had calloused my soles and toes, but I still felt the sting of ice.

"Hello?" I said, uncertainly.

The singing stopped, and a young woman emerged from between two bushes, carrying a wounded, half-grown lamb in her arms. As she stepped closer, I saw that though she looked older than Julian, she was not as old as the hunter. Not quite a woman, then, but a girl.

"Good...evening..." she said a little formally, taking in the sight of me and the doe-unicorn. I saw that she had thick, dark, curling hair like me, but braided into a sort of crown on top of her head. She was wearing a shirt and trousers of greyish white and a shearling coat. She had a satchel slung over one shoulder and she wore sheepskin boots to protect her feet from the cold.

I burst into tears. "There's a hunter. He tried to get us. We had to run away." As if in sympathy, the lamb gave out a shrill, shivering bleat. It was damp, with a bright red stain spreading over one haunch.

"*Chuu,*" the girl crooned. "There's nothing to be afraid of.

There's no one in this part of the forest." Though she had a strong, sing-song accent, she chose her words with confidence.

"Please!"

The girl's eyes flicked from the unicorn to me. "I did not see anyone. You are safe here. But my lamb is not." She knelt and laid the lamb down on the forest floor.

"What happened to you?" I asked, joining the girl beside the lamb. It was a little, pathetic thing, and obviously did not belong in the forest.

"My...sheeps...were attacked by a *zhar-turgul*."

"What's a *zhar-turgul*?"

"A...hunting bird. A bird that hunts."

"A hawk?"

She nodded. "Like a hawk, but bigger. Its name, in your tongue, means firebird." She continued. "The *zhar-turgul* picked up this little sheep, but I threw a rock and hit him. The *zhar-turgul* dropped the lamb on the other side of the river. I followed her."

River? There was a little creek by our campsite, but nothing with a strong current. Yet now, if I strained my ears, I heard something deep and rushing.

"Where's your flock now? Did the hawk get them?"

"They are safe. My friend is with them," she said simply. "I shouldn't have come after her." She patted the lamb's head. "But I did."

I peered at the lamb. Its breathing was fast and ragged. It looked as cold as I felt.

"She must be hurting from the fall," the girl said. "Not just outside, but inside, too."

I looked behind me, at the unicorn. I remembered what Mrs. Helder had said about the healing power of unicorn horns. What was it called? Alicorn?

"I think you should help her," I said to the unicorn. "The lamb is very little, so I don't think it would be hard."

My unicorn stepped forward and bent her horn to the lamb's small, shuddering chest. The little animal's breathing grew steadier and its bleating quieted. The stain seemed to dry and turn brown, as if a wound had closed. After a moment, the lamb lifted its head from the ground, stood up and shook itself. It looked at the girl expectantly, as if to say, "Now what?"

The girl gave a small, wary smile. "Thank you...I should go home now." She made to pick up her satchel, but I grabbed her wrist in panic.

"No! Don't! What about the hunter?"

Very gently, she stroked my hand to ease my grip. She ran a finger over the unicorn hair entwined between my fingers. "What's this you have here?"

"Unicorn hairs. I probably hurt her when I fell off." And, remembering the hunter gripping my hair, I began to sniffle again. The girl stroked my back.

"Don't be scared," she said with a smile. "Here, let me make you a good-luck charm." Gently unfolding my closed hand, she took three strands of unicorn mane-hairs that had tangled around my fingers and braided them together. She wrapped the cord around my wrist three times and knotted the ends. "Hold them close for a bit," she said and opened her satchel. Inside, I saw a hairy waterskin, bundles of different sorts of hardy-looking plants, something savoury-smelling in a handkerchief, and a packet of thread and needles. She bit off a length of thread with her teeth, then sewed the knot shut. "There, what do you think?" she said, with a grin.

I gave her a watery smile. "It's very pretty." I handed her the rest of the hairs wadded in my hands. "You should have these. You deserve good luck, too."

"Thank you," she said, her hand closing over them. "If you'll let me take them home, I'll do something better. I'll weave them into a magic belt and it will protect the person who wears it. A good plan, yes?"

I nodded very quickly. The girl seemed entirely magical to me already. I fell onto her and gave her a tight hug, too tight, I fear, because she very quickly unwrapped my hands from around her neck. She looked a little spooked, but I was desperate for her to like me.

"What's your name?" I said.

"It's bad luck to tell a strange creature your name." The girl laughed, but she seemed just the slightest bit uneasy.

"I'm not a strange creature!"

My answer pleased her. "Isn't that exactly what a strange creature would say?" she said, half-teasing, half-serious. "But thank you, all the same. I will leave offerings to you."

"Offerings?"

"What would you like? Milk and bread? Honey cakes?"

If she was offering me supper, I could not object. "I like all of those. Can I have them now?"

She flashed her teeth, against her better judgment, it seemed. "No, I don't have them with me."

"Do you live close by? I could come to your house."

Her smile dimmed, and she gathered her lamb into her arms. "No, let me bring them to you. I should go, before it gets dark. My mother will worry."

"Mine, too," I said with sudden realization. For some reason, that made her grin again, as if it was funny to think that I had a mother. Beside me, the unicorn knelt down for me. It was time to go, it seemed.

"If you see the hunter," I said, "be careful, please."

She laughed again, and I felt embarrassed. The unicorn turned and set into a fast walk through the dark trees. I felt the wind rise suddenly. The bushes and branches blurred around me, and I wound my fingers tightly into the unicorn's mane. I closed my eyes and felt the air grow hot with the golden-green light of a summer afternoon. When I opened them, I saw a clearing through the trees. And there it was, the pony cart.

"Ma," I shouted, "I'm back."

The unicorn trotted a few steps out of the trees but stayed in the shadows. This time, I dismounted without hurting myself. I kissed the unicorn's shoulder. "Thank you," I said, before bolting away. I had learned that Ma did not like me to dawdle around.

I ran to the pony cart where I found not just Ma, but Victor and Julian. I stopped short. There was a box of Ma's things outside the pony cart, but Ma was sitting on the pony cart's steps, straight-backed and with her arms crossed.

"Ma?" I said. When she saw me, she leapt down and embraced me. It was a fierce, almost painful hug. It was less pleasant than the mysterious girl's had seemed, but I loved Ma more. Over her shoulder, I saw Julian shoot Victor an expression of pure relief. Victor looked stern and expressionless.

"I told you she'd come back," Ma said. "Elizabeth, *where* have you been? It's been hours!"

"Then you won't come with us?" Victor said.

"How could I?"

Victor heaved a short, irritated breath. "Very well. Come along, Julian. We're not wanted here."

Ma did not correct him, though she made me curtsy to my uncle and cousin. As I spread my shift as far as it would go, Julian caught sight of the unicorn hairs woven around my wrist.

"What are those?" he said.

But I had grown suspicious within the space of an afternoon. "They're nothing," I said.

He shrugged, gave the laziest bow possible, and they rode off into the gloaming.

CHAPTER FOUR

A Little Life

The next morning, I did not understand Ma's anger. She took me to the creek and made me scrub my face and my hands. Then she sat me down on the steps of the pony cart and plaited my hair very tightly. It was only after I was dressed to her satisfaction in shirt, skirt and apron, that she started to gather twigs for the morning fire.

"Ma, I'm hungered," I said.

And she said nothing, just continued to build the pyramid of sticks.

"Ma, I'm *hungered*," I repeated, in the manner of the village children.

"You are hungry," she answered, as she struck sparks with her flint stones.

"That's what I said!"

She turned to look at me with narrowed eyes. "No. You said you were hungered. That is peasant talk."

"Pa talked like that."

"You don't belong to him. Not anymore. You are *my* daughter."

If I were older, I would have understood. Instead, I was furious at her. "Don't talk about Pa like that!"

Her thin lips twisted. "You're not the one to give orders, my dear. Go pick some firewood and cool your temper."

I stomped off, but my anger evaporated when I saw who was waiting for me. My doe-unicorn had been watching us from the side of the forest. She stepped carefully, so she could avoid the path of the campfire smoke as the breeze shifted.

I put out my hand to her. "Thank you. For yesterday."

The doe-unicorn turned her big head to the side so that she could measure the weight of my gesture with an azure eye.

Between deliveries of firewood, I tried to tempt her with the various parts of my breakfast: an apple, a bowl of oat porridge, a wizened carrot. She did not want any of them. Instead, she waited for me to come back empty-handed. Then, she led me into the trees, where another doe and dappled fawn watched me from the shadows. Whereas my doe-unicorn had a long, fierce horn, the mother had a mere bud peeping from her forelock, still covered in velvet, like the emergent antlers of young deer. The gangly fawn's forehead was bare, but it was recognizable as a unicorn because of its cloven hooves and the elegant curves of its muzzle.

I stepped forward eagerly. The mother-doe turned away, trotted a few steps and then looked behind to see if I was following. I jogged along behind them, hopping over fallen logs and trying not to trip on roots. In the forest, the air smelled new and the stippled sunlight made the grey unicorns almost invisible.

Suddenly, the mother-doe stopped and circled around. Tired after the run, the fawn dipped its head under its mother's belly and suckled from her teat. The mother-doe pawed the loam with her cloven hoof and shook her head.

My doe-unicorn nudged me hard between the shoulder blades. I approached slowly. There, where the mother-doe had scraped the fallen leaves, I saw the ivory spiral of a horn. Alicorn. The mother-doe was giving me hers. She must have shed her alicorn when her fawn was born and regrown it afterwards. I picked it up and thanked them. The mother-doe blinked slowly, as if to say it didn't matter. I suppose she hadn't any use for a shed horn. But I did.

I ran back home with the horn in my outstretched arms, my anger at Ma forgotten.

"Ma, look!" I crowed. Ma frowned as she looked up from stirring our lunch (barley soup, for a change), but her irritation vanished when she saw what I carried.

She embraced me and kissed my temple. "What a clever girl you are!"

I settled into her body, then looked at the pot. "Is lunch ready? I'm fashed!"

She tweaked my braid a little harder than was necessary. "You are *famished*, Elizabeth. The women in our family are never fashed *or* hungered."

A week later, Nicholas Helder brought us a box from the village. Mrs. Helder brought us a fat pigeon pie and jam tarts. Though I had not seen anyone in the forest since Julian and Victor's visit, the memory of the hunter was still fresh in my mind. I thought that Mrs. Helder must have gossiped about what I had found and that her stories must have sent the hunter my way. As we watched as Nicholas helped Ma pry the box open, I kept my eyes on Ma. I did not meet Mrs. Helder's smile.

When the nails in the packing crate gave way with a creak, we found a letter in fluid, curling script lying on top of packing straw. Ma read it aloud:

"Dear Sister. Please consider this your portion of the inheritance. Mother is still alive, but she does not wish you to embarrass the family dignity by returning after her death. Upon much solemn meditation, I have taken the liberty of sending a few additional items for the child. If she can be educated to the appropriate level, the family may once more extend the hand of kindness."

Inside, nestled in the straw, was a set of glass flasks, glass rods, iron stands, a mortar and pestle, and a set of heavy clay cups that

Ma said were crucibles. There was also a small chest filled with even smaller drawers that opened to reveal dried herbs, pebbly bits of fragrant resin, vials of desiccated beetles. Underneath all of this was a set of leather-bound books, embossed with a coat of armour—a rose and three feathers—with crackling pages of vellum, rather than linen paper. Ma's nose wrinkled as she read. "*A Ladies Legacie to her Daughters, The Schoole of Good Manners*...he must have raided our nursery. Solemn meditation, indeed! *The History of the Kings of Gersa*...that'll be for your schooling, too, Elizabeth. Ah, this looks better...*The Almanack of Four-Footed Beastes*. And here we are. *The Herbarium and Bestiary of Camilla Alacoque*." She looked up at me and smiled thinly. It seemed that these glass flasks and books, as much as my alicorn, were what she had been waiting for.

But before she could set to work, the Helders insisted on sharing their food with us. When Mrs. Helder held out a slice of pigeon pie, I crossed my arms and would not look at her.

"Behave, Elizabeth!" said Ma, in frosty disbelief. *The mark of a good parent*, I remembered Victor saying, *is the character of the child*. I was shaming her...but it was Mrs. Helder who ought to feel sorry.

"Why, Elizabeth, what's happened?" Mrs. Helder reached out and touched my arm, very gently.

I jerked away from her. "You told people about the unicorn, didn't you?"

"Upon my soul, I swear I have not! What's happened?"

I glanced at Mrs. Helder and saw incomprehension on her face. She had not told? But then, how? I told them about the hunter. "He knew my name," I said. "He said I was the one who found unicorns."

Mrs. Helder's rosy cheeks paled. "I swear," she repeated, "I never told a soul. Could it be he saw you that first night?"

"I don't know," I said. "At least the girl was nice."

"What girl?" Mrs. Helder said slowly.

When I described her, the last of Mrs. Helder's smile faded. I wasn't sure why. "I liked her lamb. And she said she would give me honey cakes. And it was almost winter there," I added.

"Elizabeth, you aren't making this up?" Ma said abruptly.

"No, what would I make up?" The girl had looked completely ordinary. Curly dark hair. Dark eyes.

"Well...well, she looks just like you."

I giggled at the thought. "No...She was almost grown up!"

"It may be," Mrs. Helder said, "that she took the form she thought you might trust most. She might have seen you from afar and taken your shape."

My mouth hung open at the thought. "Was she Old Folk?" I asked. "An elf-lady? A ghost?"

Mrs. Helder pursed her lips. "Perhaps. She might have tried to lure you. You might have been in great danger. She might have wanted to steal your body. There're stories of changelings, you see? Sometimes people wander in, and when they come out, they're never quite the same. Oh, their faces are the same, but there's something, as if behind the eyes, that's changed. As if another creature is living there."

No. That didn't sound at all like the girl I had met. "But she was mostly worried about the lamb! She didn't *want* me to get too near her!"

"Elizabeth, you must be careful."

Nicholas Helder harrumphed, and we all turned to him. "Mam, look at you, taken in by a child's stories."

"It's not a story! It happened!"

"Did it? And did you tell your mother?"

I looked quickly at Ma, whose mouth was a prim, straight line. She had been too angry at Victor for me to say anything, and after, when I found the alicorn, I had only wanted her to be happy. But somehow, I didn't think this explanation would convince Nicholas. "I didn't want to scare her," I said, quietly.

"See, Mam? She's telling you because she knows she can spook you!"

I couldn't say anything to defend myself. I hunched my shoulders and looked down. Mrs. Helder gave my arm a pat. "See what you've done, Nicholas? You've hurt her feelings. I believe you, kitten, not to worry. Just be watchful when you wander, understand?"

But Mrs. Helder's words only made me determined to go back. If I had seen an elf-girl and a ghost *and* unicorns, I might find Pa, too.

Wanting to find Pa was an ambition I struggled to fulfil. Ma kept a close eye on me, at first. In the afternoons and evenings, I had lessons from *A Ladies Legacie to her Daughters* and the other books Victor sent us, and Ma never ceased to correct my speech. I didn't mind my lessons because Ma also taught me to write up what I learned about the forest plants. In the mornings, after we tended the garden, I went exploring or foraging for mushrooms and herbs and tried to find the unicorns. Occasionally, I would stumble upon an old piece of alicorn hiding here or there in the loam and pick it up.

Sometimes, I caught glimpses of the hunter, middle-aged and sharpening a spear, or an old man pottering around a bark hut. I learned to avoid those parts of the forest. Or else I'd find a unicorn along the way to the hunter's haunts, and they'd lead me to something interesting or useful—a cluster of restharrow or henbane, a patch of wild strawberries. I could not find Pa, and I stopped looking for him. As I grew older, I also thought less about the girl with the lamb, whom I never saw again.

The unicorns, my silent strangers, set the pace of my new

life. Where they went, I followed. When I was a bit older, I began to wander, carrying a bag with flint and tinder, an oil-skin sheet and blanket and some provisions of fat, dried meat and oats in case of overnight excursions. I was always searching for newly shed horns because we discovered that fresher horns healed wounds more swiftly. After the winter solstice, the older bucks' horns dropped off. Then, in the early summer, the does shed their horns before they dropped their fawns so that they could nuzzle them without hurting their young. The does and fawns grew their horns slowly throughout the summer. By the next spring, the yearlings' first horns would grow in. Day by day, the yearlings' growing alicorn pushed them further from fawn-hood; many were chased away after accidentally pricking their mothers' sides in a vain attempt to reach the teat. That was when their lives as adults began.

I found the alicorn and Ma experimented with it, with her crucibles and flasks. Mostly, she made an ointment out of it. Rub it into a cut—it would scab within minutes and soon the scab would dry and flake off. If the cut was small, the ointment would leave no scar behind. Rub it into a wrenched shoulder—the muscle loosened and ceased to ache. When we visited the village to sell the ointment, though, we did not mention uni-corns. My first brush with the hunter—ghost or not—had been enough. We did not want poachers, and Ma wished to keep the recipe secret. We kept our prices low, but we kept ourselves safe.

It was several years before I saw anything strange in the forest.

CHAPTER FIVE

The Hunter

I was sixteen by then and distracted by the task of raising Sida, my unicorn fawn.

By the time Sida arrived, we lived in a rough log house, and a mule grazed next to the pony cart, waiting for Ma's next trip to Wealdton's market day or further up to Bartlieu Fair and beyond, where she could command a higher price. Except for the Helders, we lived very much alone. Ma had not discouraged the rumours that she might be a witch—a white witch who cast a shadow of variable grey. As for me? Well, Ma's manner of talking might win her respect, but it won me no friends. I was both uppity and a witch's brat; only the local girls' and boys' fear of Ma kept me safe. So, when Sida tottered out of the forest in early spring, I was glad to have an excuse to stay home.

Sida had come to me escorted by a yearling doe. Not her mother, I saw by the doe's tight, milkless teats and her quick retreat into the undergrowth. Where the mother had gone was impossible to say. Probably dead, though the yearling doe never led me to a body. Unicorns, I have noticed, maintain a distance, so that we have only what they choose to give us.

But Sida was different, because she was so little. She was frail, and her skin was loose on her bones. She would not suckle on our nanny goat, but if I dipped a rag in a bucket, she would accept the milk from me. When the first critical phase of keeping her alive had passed, Sida followed me around the garden and the house. I liked to keep my hand on her head, between her ears, as I went from bed to kitchen, from kitchen to garden. We walked in step with each other.

That day, I held Sida in my lap, with her spindly legs nearly reaching the ground. I held her tight to my chest because Ma was going to leave me later that morning for a trading journey. Again.

She needed to go—she needed to sell, so we could thrive—but I was upset. So, on impulse, I picked a fight once the pony cart was packed and she was putting on what she called her "costume."

"A certain reputation is good for business, Elizabeth," she explained as she hooked silver bangles into her earlobes, "and I will look my part." She leaned toward the mirror to examine the thin lines that had recently appeared across her forehead and at the corners of her eyes and mouth.

"Can you bring me some earrings, too?" I asked. Sida slid out of my lap and gamboled over to the cold fireplace. I let her go, knowing she'd come back soon.

The lines on Ma's face deepened as she frowned before responding. "These earrings, Elizabeth, are for my part of the business. You don't need them. Earrings are not what other people need to see on you." Sida began nosing around in last night's ashes.

"I don't need to be seen at all. You don't want me to see anything, either. I never go anywhere. You make me read books about the wonders of the world, but you won't let me go look at it," I said bitterly.

Ma gave a hum as she attempted to suppress her scorn. "Bartlieu Fair is hardly one of the 'wonders of the world.'"

"Fine, how should I know? Ma, why can't I come with you? Together, we could sell twice as much."

"And Sida?"

"Sida can trot beside the mule or rest in the cart."

Ma raised an eyebrow. I'd recently used Sida's health as an

excuse not to visit Mrs. Helder on market day. I hadn't wanted to face the unfriendly faces of the village lads and lasses.

Now, however, I wanted to get far away. Even though I loved the forest, in this moment, its familiarity was stifling. I pressed on. "It's like you want me to be alone all the time, like some sort of hermit."

"If you want to put it that way," Ma agreed sternly. "You're much better off here than in the village or on the road, and you know it." Now her eyes caught on Sida. My fawn lay down and began rolling back and forth, smearing her lovely dappled coat with soot.

"*Must* you keep that animal in the house?" Ma said. She never had the same affection for the unicorns as I did. Sometimes, I wondered if Ma found the unicorns interesting only because they produced a rare medicinal ingredient.

There was a knock at the door.

The surprise of the sound made Sida leap up and retreat into Ma's workplace. With a cry of dismay, Ma ran after her. "Get the door, Elizabeth!"

I went to open it, expecting Mrs. Helder and a basket of pasties.

Hunter, was my first thought. And then I silently corrected myself. *Rich* hunter.

In his hands, he held the reins of a gleaming, blood bay stallion, and the tooled burgundy leather of its bridle and saddle exactly matched his velvet hunting suit. This man had a long, curled, iridescent red-gold plume stretching back from the folds of his flat velvet cap. The village lads sometimes stuck feathers in the crown of their hats—cockerels' tails and the pinfeathers of geese if they were homely types, pheasant or eagle feathers if they hunted. This feather reminded me of the firebird the elf-girl had described, an animal I hadn't ever seen. I doubted this man had collected the feather from the creature itself. But my heart squeezed at the thought of Sida. What if he saw her?

"Hello, Elizabeth," he said with a white-toothed smile.

The stranger looked me up and down with indolence, as if I were a toad when he had been hoping for a dragon. I stared back. A crossbow and quiver of bolts gently clinked together on one side of his stallion, while on the other, I saw the long muzzle of an arquebus. Nicholas Helder had told me about them, how they were used to blow men apart on faraway battlefields. This arquebus must be for show, not use—they were horribly inaccurate and very expensive.

I heard Ma opening our side door—the one that led from Ma's study to the garden. If she was shooing Sida out, then this man must come in.

"Would you like to step inside, sir? My mother can give you directions to the nearest town."

He smiled and bowed in a graceful sweep. "You don't remember me? Your cousin, Julian."

Something flickered through my memory, but it wasn't simply matching this self-satisfied creature with his obnoxious younger self.

Why was he here? Behind the young man, I saw the familiar, black-coated figure of Victor, perched on his palomino mare.

"Ah, Victor," Ma said, arriving behind me with a forced smile. She was wiping her sooty hands into her apron. Sida had sullied her clothes, and Ma never wanted to appear dirty. Especially in front of Victor.

As I ushered in our guests, I saw Sida digging in the garden, throwing dirt up onto her haunches. I hoped she'd cover herself completely while Victor and Julian were inside.

We shared a stilted conversation over a late-morning meal. Our diet had improved greatly as I learned to match the pictures

in Ma's herbarium to the plants I foraged. I served yesterday's
oatcakes with wild strawberry jam and birch syrup, and soft
goat's cheese crusted with wild thyme on bread. Victor and
Julian watched me as I set out the plates and dished out the por-
tions. When they asked me questions, my answers were clear
and short. I wanted them to state their business and be gone—
I didn't like the idea of them meeting Sida. Julian kept staring at
me and I wished he wouldn't. When they were done eating, and
before I cleared the plates, Victor cleared his throat.

"Elizabeth, your mother and I have been discussing your
future."

"When?"

Victor looked from Ma to me. "We met recently at Bartlieu
Fair."

That had been less than two weeks ago, and she hadn't said
a thing. "Ma?"

"Victor, this isn't what we discussed. I have not had time to…"

"Look, Sylvia, I don't mean to be cruel, but we don't *have*
time. Remember what I said about Mother."

"Go on, then." Her voice was dry.

"I did not understand why you were at the market, but I have
since found out." Victor set a jar of ointment on the table in front
of us. "Sylvia, you have become…known…in these parts."

"Have you tried it?"

"Yes." The admission seemed to pain him. "It is very effec-
tive, very useful." He cleared his throat.

"But…"

"It would not be seemly to accept you back into the family
when you have become…"

"Say it, Victor."

His eyes flicked to her sooty apron. "Common. Coarse.
A peddler."

"She isn't just a peddler," I burst out. "She helps heal people all over the county." In saying this, I was leaving out not only my work, but our utter dependence on tracking, finding and befriending the unicorns. "Some people call her a miracle worker!"

"Or a witch," Victor returned lightly. "And it would harm the family's reputation to have a witch in the family."

"How can a witch be common? Witches are *un*common."

He ignored me and turned to Ma. "But I am pleased to see your progress with Elizabeth. Her manner is still slightly...raw, but she's a credit to you. She could be salvaged and shaped. As I said, we would be willing to take her. Just her."

"You don't know me!"

"Elizabeth, keep quiet! Victor is offering you a chance at a better life."

"Better?" Before Victor had arrived, I had been chafing to escape and Ma had restrained me. Now, given the opportunity, I was flinging it away. After all, I had Ma and I had Sida. "Ma, *you* left! Why should I be sent back to a life you ran away from?"

"I was a young fool, Elizabeth. Don't be like me. I'd much rather have you raised properly. You could have an education."

"For what?"

"If we're lucky," Julian quipped, stroking his dark moustache and beard, "we'll be able to marry you off to a merchant of decent standing. A step up from a tinker, at least."

I glared at him, and he smiled back at me. I turned to Ma. "But...but what about..." She couldn't continue the business without me. She needed me! Sida needed me, and Ma knew that, too.

"We will provide your mother with an allowance that will keep her comfortable."

"You'd pay her to give me up? Ma, you're *selling* me?"

"I am willing to sacrifice my small success to see you returned to your rightful place."

"What if *this* is my rightful place?" I had a talent with the unicorns, a gift. If I left, I'd just be the poor relation.

She lifted an eyebrow. "Trust me, it isn't."

"Just say it. You don't want me!"

She gave a snort and I stormed out. I'd go to the forest. I'd take Sida—what would they do then? I kicked open the thatched gate to our garden, and Sida, startled, stopped her digging. Her eyes were wide and scared. "Sorry, girl," I said, and I bent over and stretched out a hand to her. She was spattered from head to cloven hooves in mud. She trotted towards me, but when I stepped backwards, towards the gate, she circled around and hid behind the frames where I'd trained the marrow squash to grow. She did not like my temper. She would not come to me while I was angry. So, I knelt in the dirt and began to weed beside the runner beans, hoping Sida would come to see what I was doing.

Gardening is mucky work, and when your ma is my Ma, you put on your raggediest clothes for the task. I usually wore the breeches that I took out into the forest, but today I had no choice. I might as well get dirty and show Victor and Julian just how unsuited I was to be adopted. I picked the plantago and pennycress and purslane and lamb's quarters threatening my rows of hardy cabbage, beets, beans. But still, Sida peeped at me from behind the squash frames.

The front door opened and closed quietly, and steps rustled towards the garden. Sida ducked behind the broad squash leaves. I didn't look over my shoulder, but I was ready for Ma to apologize.

"*Dear* Elizabeth." Julian's voice was cool, ironic.

I turned my head to look at him but stayed crouched by my runner beans. I prayed for Sida to keep herself hidden. He had his arquebus slung over his shoulder, and he was fanning himself with his handsome gloves. The gold rings on his fingers glinted. It was midday, and the sun beat down on us. My shadow was pooled underneath me, protecting my toes.

"I'm not going," I said.

"Have no fear—*I* don't want you." But his tone was displeased, as if I had failed to respond to his glory. Then he cleared his throat, and when he spoke again, he thought he was unctuous and inviting. "But Elizabeth, I've heard that marvellous creatures live in these woods."

"Who told you?" I spoke angrily. I hoped my sharp tone would keep Sida wary. What would Julian do if he saw her?

He laughed. "No one had to tell me. Fenlen Forest is… known. Stories, curious tales in old books."

I should have laughed him off or bored him with a lecture on our humble collection of herbs. But I was Ma's daughter, and my sullen face told him I knew something.

"Do you remember the day we met? You came out of the forest wearing a bracelet of, well, rather odd animal hair."

I glowered at him and covered my wrist. Since my encounter with the strange girl, I had a habit of braiding unicorn hairs and wearing them. Now I wished I'd taken them off. But Julian saw, and his smile widened.

Look anywhere but his eyes, or at where I thought Sida might be, I told myself. My eyes caught on his stupid hat and the iridescent red-gold feather stuck into it. He saw where I looked and stroked his plumage with a pompous finger. "This is the tail feather of a firebird I shot northeast of here. A species related to the phoenix, you know. I have a reputation as a rather talented hunter of exotic breeds." I had no response to his foul boast, and his voice rolled on. "So, the question remains: what strange beasties do you keep around here?"

And that was when Sida coughed quietly. I looked over. She was trying to eat a squash leaf that was much too big for her. But if Julian noticed Sida.... "Is that a dwarf mule?" he asked. "What an ugly creature it is!" His eyes were on Sida. "Unless..."

I needed to keep his attention on me, away from Sida. "My mule's not as ugly as you." Ladies probably thought he was handsome, I thought. Even features, full lips, broad shoulders. I stood up suddenly.

He opened the gate to my garden. "When Uncle Victor showed me your mother's ointment, I was sure that she was using alicorn," he said. He stepped on one of my beet plants.

"Be careful!" I stepped backwards, trying to block Sida from his line of sight. I heard Sida circle around, nervously kicking into the young cabbage.

"Or else?" We stood staring at each other. I had mud on my knees and under my nails and he had the power to take Sida away, or to take *me* away, and to destroy my garden. That flicker of fear in my eyes was all he needed to see. "Come on," he coaxed, "tell me where they are..."

"Do *you* see any unicorns here?" I said. "No. So go away."

His lip curled, the smile changed subtly. "I've heard that if you tie a maiden to a tree..."

I took a cautious step back. At least he wasn't paying any attention to Sida now. "I won't do anything to please you."

"Come now, it won't hurt." He grabbed at me.

I turned on my heel and ran.

I heard him smashing through my garden as I jumped the fence on the far side. Good. As long as he was coming after me, he was leaving Sida alone. His heavy clothing slowed him down, but he was strongly built. I sped along the stream's bank but realized he would track me there. I leapt over it and ran blindly through the undergrowth, over fallen trees. I could no longer hear the sounds of the clearing. Somewhere behind me, I heard the bugling call of a unicorn. I couldn't tell whether it was meant to guide me, or whether it had been surprised by Julian.

I scrambled up a rocky ledge, scraping my knees badly as I climbed. I ducked behind a big linden and paused. I couldn't hear him anymore. I steadied my breathing, listening hard for any trace of movement. Nothing—just the fluting song of an oriole.

Was I safe? I wasn't sure. But Sida was safe. That was the important point.

Leaning back against the tree, I looked around. I'd never been in this part of the forest, I thought, though I couldn't have gone that far. The trees were younger, more widely spaced apart. The sun shone warmly through the thin, shifting canopy. The breeze was warm, but as I nestled in between the roots, I began to shiver. My shirt was damp from running and from fear.

I waited and waited, listening for the heavy footsteps of a well-fed man.

But I heard nothing.

Worried that my limbs would get stiff, I stood up and rubbed my arms and legs. I'd need to get home, but other than climbing down the ledge, I didn't have a sharp sense of where to go. I couldn't head home the way I'd come. If Julian had any sense, he'd turn back to the lip of the forest and wait for me to return. But then he might see Sida. But as long as Sida was dirty, he wouldn't recognize her.

I followed the sloping ledge, stretching my arms as I went. The forest looked very different from this angle. Though I had passed through old trees, *now* the place I had run from looked like new growth. Instead of dead leaves between the trees, there was long, silky grass. How odd. I nearly forgot my fear of Julian, when I heard the thud-thud-thud of hooves. Unshod hooves, soft in their fall.

I looked up to see the old doe-unicorn, my first. She still frightened me, a little, but I respected her more. For that reason, in all our years together, I had not given her any silly nicknames like I had to others. She was not a Dilly (fond of the herb) or a Diamond (a young child's idea of sophistication). And, of course, she was not at all like Sida. I had never tried to tame my scar-shouldered unicorn. She was her own, silent self. She trotted right up to me and around my back. She was going to lead me home.

I did not talk to her or tell her about what had happened. I didn't think she'd be interested in understanding. She liked me, I knew, but I was not where she thought I should be. We walked in silence. I wondered how she saw the forest, how she knew where to go.

Her nostrils quivered and we veered to the left. I also tried smelling the air deeply. My nose, a bit runny from my exertions, gave a wet snuffle. The unicorn stopped to stare at me severely.

"Sorry," I said quickly, and she continued walking. I needed to get home and hide Sida before Julian returned.

My nose caught the thick smell of damp moss. We were making our way into older-growth forest, where the trees grew close together and the ground was soft with the damp, crumbling remnants of old trunks and stumps. Above us, the leaves were thick, blocking out the sun. My toe snagged on something and I fell over, yelping as the grit of the forest floor got into my skinned knees. The unicorn stopped patiently and waited for me to pick myself up.

I turned to see what I had fallen over, thinking it might be alicorn because I saw an ivory, domed shape. There was a space underneath it—that's where my toe had caught. I hooked my finger under it and pulled. After another tug, the soft earth gave away.

I found myself holding a human skull by one, empty eye socket. Behind me, the unicorn sighed, impatient, resigned.

After the first jolt of shock, I felt my pulse calm. This was an old, old piece of bone, most of it stained different shades of brown from its exposure. It was smooth and there were bits of leaf mold under my fingernails when I unhooked them from the socket. Old enough to be buried by nature and to be uncovered by rain and wind. I ran my hand into the cavity in the earth, looking for a snatch of fabric that might have told me about its owner. Nothing there. But the doe-unicorn pawed at the ground and I saw a glint of something. I picked up a thick, gold ring. A man's ring. Rather like the one Julian had worn this morning and like that of the strange hunter who had attacked me years ago. I felt my heart squeeze in fear.

I put the skull back quickly and covered it with leaves. I was imagining things. He'd gone back. I'd arrive in our clearing and find him taunting our mule. I'd shout at him for chasing me and I'd refuse to live with him and Victor. Yes. That was what had happened. That was what I would do. But I slipped the ring into my pocket, nonetheless.

The unicorn was kneeling when I turned around. I was to climb onto her because I had wasted enough time already, her eyes seemed to tell me. I wound my hands into her mane and she set off at a trot. Soon, we were on more familiar trails. She sped into a canter when we found the stream and we burst out into the sunshine.

Julian was not waiting for me. He was not standing in the meadow grass or watching Sida as she nibbled on carrot fronds.

My doe-unicorn would not stay to be groomed or to snack on my trodden garden. She did not even seem to notice Sida, who was hiding under a toppled row of beans. Instead, she trotted over to Julian's blood bay stallion and, with a few prods of her horn, undid the simple knot that secured its reins to our hitching post. The stallion, proud animal though he was, took one glance at her and galloped up the hill in the other direction.

Then, my doe-unicorn nipped at my shoulder and took herself back into the forest. For a human, her pace would have been a boastful saunter; for a horse, it would have been a prance.

I looked at my garden. Ma and Victor would be angry at me, of course. I had been gone several hours, no doubt. Or had I? It had been shadowless noon when Julian had stepped on my plants, but now the shade had barely started peeping over the eastern side of the house. The weeds I picked had only just started to wilt. Sida sniffed at them and lightly vaulted over the garden fence.

Sida followed me as I washed off my wounds in the stream. Most of the dirt and soot ran off her downy fur, but she was still a dull brown-grey. We cautiously approached the house and entered the side door to my mother's workshop. In the main room, I could hear the murmur of Ma's and Victor's voices. If I had been gone long, they would have run out of things to say. If Julian had arrived back, he would have been adding his own sardonic twist on my disappearance. I hated him.

Quietly, I scrounged around my mother's workshop for the household pot of ointment. I dabbed it on my knees and the palms of my hands. My skin itched a little as scabs formed and dried where shredded flesh had been. In a few minutes, I'd absentmindedly scratch them off when I gave Sida a pat—and find healthy new skin in their place.

I replaced the jar, careful not to disturb my mother's piles of notes for the syrup she was developing. For internal complaints, alicorn was tricky because it tasted chalky and stuck to the back of your throat. Instead of getting it into your body, you'd cough most of it up. If I reshuffled her papers, I might set us back by months.

"Elizabeth, is that you?" Ma called.

"Yes, Ma," I said. I went to the inner door of the workshop and entered the main cabin. I breathed in and looked at Victor. "Thank you for offering to take me in, but I can't."

"Hmmm," said Victor, looking me up and down. Now I looked as dirty, as coarse, as my mother. A lost cause.

I turned to Ma. "I do not want to stay where Julian is. He…" I tried to order my thoughts. "I do not *like* him."

Ma's forehead creased. I very seldom disobeyed her. "But, Elizabeth…"

"I don't feel safe with him." I crossed my arms and saw that my dishevelled clothes and raw hands did not escape her notice.

"I wouldn't want to send you where…" Her eyes flicked to Victor. "Would you anticipate him causing trouble?"

"Well, yes." He looked around, as if to register Julian's reaction. "Where is that boy?"

I shrugged. "I saw him heading off to the forest," I said. That was, as far as I knew, true.

"The young fool," Victor swore. "He said he wanted to go off hunting."

When he went outside to investigate, Victor of course found Julian's blood bay stallion gone and no trace of Julian himself. "Julian mentioned there's good hunting a bit north from here," Victor said. "He must have gone that way."

There was nothing I could say, though I felt the ring heavy in my skirt pocket. Victor gave his sister a dry kiss on the cheek and departed. That night, as Ma was in her workshop and Sida slept by my bedside, I took out *The Schoole of Good Manners*. I compared the embossed leather cover with the ring I had found. The crest of a rose and three feathers, one tooled into calfskin, the other etched into gold. I ran out of the house and flung the ring as far as I could into the trees. I didn't want any part of

Julian near me. My old, scarred doe disappeared after that day. At first, I did not remark upon her absence, because the unicorns came and went according to their own plans. And, after all, I had Sida, who started coming with me into Fenlen Forest. I was happier amongst the trees than at the house.

After Victor left, Ma became bitter. She never forgot to remind me that I had chosen wrong. No effort I made was good enough. I collected plants and began my own herbarium. I made bilberry jam for receding, bleeding gums. I invented a recipe for burdock-root fritters for costive bowels and brewed an elderberry cordial for coughs.

"But why would I sell these housewife's concoctions," my mother said when I suggested she bring a few samples on her next trip, "when alicorn heals all these remedies with more lasting effect?" I gathered bright birds' feathers and strips of shed unicorn velvet and shining unicorn hair from the branches of trees. Ma had laughed at the lumpy rug that I braided out of unicorn velvet.

"What does that protect against?" she had said. "Muddy floors? I think other rugs do that as well."

I struggled to convince Ma that by choosing her, I had chosen rightly. I tried to show her that our life was good. And I tended Sida. She let me baby her and pretend that she was tame, though she was not tame. I gave her pet names, though she was not my pet at all.

This was my life; these were my ambitions.

I was seventeen when the forest took me.

CHAPTER SIX

Hide and Seek

My hope that Sida was tame, I think, was at the root of my disaster. Over the summer, autumn and winter, I watched her develop from a frail fawn to a robust yearling on the verge of growing her first horn. I did not expect her to be, well, *domestic*, but I did hope that she might stay. Sida gave me a reasonable excuse to turn down Mrs. Helder's increasingly insistent offers that I come in for market days and stay for the dances that followed.

"Why spend an evening being ignored by young farmers and shopkeepers?" I said. "I could be testing whether Sida likes eating celandines or asters, now that she's rejecting oats."

"Once Sida can find her own fodder, you'll come with me," Mrs. Helder said. Silently, I denied that such a day would come. A secret, dark part of me hoped that the goat's milk that I raised Sida on would cause her to develop more slowly.

But as her muscles grew strong under her loose baby skin, she grew impatient with me. Sida was beginning to bud her first horn and she wanted to roam the forest. And yet she would not simply leave me behind. She would scamper ahead just far enough to know that I was running after her. At first it was just the meadow around our log house, then around the mouth of the path that I took into the forest. Every day the process of singing her name and cajoling her to my side was becoming longer.

At last, in earliest spring, when the first pale shoots emerged from the retreating snow that clung to the bases of the trees and my mother had just set off on her first trip of the year, it happened.

We were on my usual trail in search of horns and my pack was heavy with supplies enough for a day and a night. I paused, stooped to look at something that might be alicorn, when Sida gave a little rear and galloped off. I dropped what had turned out to be a spiralled snail shell and ran after her. But Sida had discovered her strength and was taking joy in the ease with which she leapt over fallen tree trunks and kicked up the half-frozen moss. I could hear her snorts and calls of happiness.

When I found her again, it was dark and I had no choice but to pitch camp for the evening. Sida lay down beside me and put her head in my lap. She looked up at me and blinked repentantly. The advantage of sleeping amongst unicorns is that they are better than a fire for keeping warm on a cold spring night. You can lean into their dense winter coats and let their heat seep through you, if they let you.

"Sida," I told her in a stern voice that I had learned from Ma, "one day you are going to run off and I won't be able to follow you. Do you want that? Do you think you are old enough to be alone?" I forgave and fell asleep running my fingers through the fuzz of her cheeks.

In the morning, she had left me again. Unicorns step carefully and are hard to track, but Sida was young and silly. She admired herself too much *not* to leave her cloven hoofprints in fresh mud and rub her horn bud against the new bark of trees. She was excited with the idea of freedom and had left the paths we used to follow. The snow was deeper here than at home. I was getting cold and my food was running out. But I was more worried for Sida and paid more attention to her trail than to where I was headed.

It was late afternoon when I saw her, and we were farther

from home than I had ever been. We had been in a valley the evening before and I had moved uphill all day. The climb had levelled into a plateau, where I could see the sky through the trees.

And suddenly, there I saw her, my fawn, framed by two tall alders. The setting sun made her down glow the colour of a ripe peach. The ground tilted down sharply behind her.

"Sida!" I called. "Come here, darling."

Sida looked at me and cocked her head to one side.

I reached towards her, hand closed loosely as if I had a treat. "Sida, be a good girl. We've been gone long enough already. Mrs. Helder doesn't like it when I haven't milked the goats."

Sida nickered, pawed the ground. I took a step. She held her ground. I took another step, faster now, and a twig snapped underfoot. Sida gave a little neigh, turned and leapt.

I ran. I ran and saw the drop, but Sida was not below. It was steep, I reasoned against my panic, but not impossible to survive such a fall. Perhaps I could not see her in the snow. I called the fawn's name. Below me the trees grew at sharp angles. I clung to them as I stepped from outcrop to outcrop of tangled, bare roots.

As I fought my way down, I missed that shift in sound I always felt in my ears when I entered the forest at home. The momentary, silent pressure, like ducking your head in a stream and feeling the water against your ears. I was too worried about Sida to notice.

When I reached the bottom, I looked through the bushes. I felt the blood beat against my eardrums as I searched for a white, crumpled body, snapped legs desecrated by mud. But as the light faded from red to purple to an ever-deepening blue, I could not find her. The trees became interspersed with large granite boulders that cast innumerable shadows. As the stars started to emerge from the dark, a cold, cutting wind rose. I realized that not only was Sida lost, but I had no way of finding my way home.

If Mrs. Helder had been beside me, I would have broken into loud, wailing, messy tears. But alone, I only managed one dry, racking sob. Sida had left me and I was alone. I was alone and my unicorns had not come to comfort me. The night would be harsh and cold. And tomorrow it would be a long, weary trek home—even if I *could* find home. My fingertips were already numb and I tucked my hands under my arms as I stumbled forward, no longer looking around me. I knew I had to find a place to camp, but that meant giving up.

"*Bettina!*"

Shocked at the sound of a human voice, I turned.

"*Bettina, ti vog?*"

There was more that I could not understand, but those three words repeated again. In the dimming light, I saw a young man sitting on a large, sloping boulder, looking as scared as I did. His shoulders were tensed, and his fingers gripped into the lichen. His light grey coat and breeches were so close in colour to the dirty spring snow that he almost looked a part of the landscape. He seemed long-limbed, and the fading light emphasized the angularity of his face. He had light hair, a flyaway halo of dandelion fluff. A pale beard whose wispiness across his high cheeks suggested that he was close to my age.

"*Bettina, galan ti vog?*" His voice was tight with fear and sadness and...something else. He scrutinized my face and then passed briefly over my arms hugging my body, the leaf debris clinging to my knees, my muddy boots.

When his eyes returned to my face, I caught his gaze and realized with a shock that he desired me. Not casually, not greedily; his need for me was part of him. I felt my cheeks grow warm. I had never seen longing so openly written on anyone's face. It made me feel shy, rather than frightened.

Staring into my eyes, he shifted and knelt forward, extending his hand. "*Ni resi, Bettina, Ya vogmi.*"

"I...I don't understand you," I said slowly.

At the sound of my words, the hand retreated, as if stung. But he kept staring.

"I am sorry," I added, stepping forward. My throat was dry, and my voice was ragged. "I can't understand you."

He broke away from my gaze and looked up into the night sky. The silence stretched out. His sharp chin still lifted, but his eyes slid carefully across my hair, my mouth, my nose and finally, my eyes. He exhaled slowly.

"My apologies." He pronounced Gersan slowly and in a strange way, as if the sounds formed only at the front of his mouth. "I..." his language failed him. "You look as a girl I know." He corrected himself clumsily. "Know-*ed*." He winced, sensing that he had not expressed his meaning correctly.

"Where is she?"

He tilted his head down to look at me and spoke without answering my question. "It is strange. I do not like to, but it is...I must." He sat back out of his kneel, slid off the boulder. He picked up a tall staff with a curved top from the base of the boulder and gestured to a narrow path I had not seen, leading through the scattered rocks. "Come."

I paused. *Stay away from strangers*, I remembered Mrs. Helder saying, long ago. I remembered her fear when I told her of the girl with the lamb, who had appeared and disappeared so suddenly. Had I been too trusting then? And here I was again in the forest with a person foreign to my understanding. But the night was coming on. It would be too dark to gather firewood and I could easily freeze. *There are legends of people wandering into that forest.* He knew Gersan, I reasoned. But any clever creature might learn Gersan, I surmised with equal reason. Coming upon an eerie-looking young man at dusk was not auspicious. But he had looked shocked and mournful, rather than crafty.

And whether I went with him or not, I might be dead within hours from the cold.

The young man sensed my hesitation. "My..." he thought of the word, "my uncle. He speak...em...he speak-s Gersan." He flushed at his pronunciation, as though he expected to be chastised.

"You speak Gersan," I said.

He shook his head. "Not like him. Come, it is late. My... aunt...she has food." I approached him but kept an arm's length between us. He seemed to understand that I was nervous. Still, he kept looking at me and considering me, as if to make sure I was real.

We walked together.

"My name, Torun," he said, placing his long, narrow, outstretched fingers on his chest. He lifted that hand off and gestured at me, his calloused palm forming a question.

"Elizabeth."

He looked at me sharply.

"Yes?" I said.

"Elizabeth, Bettina. Same name." Torun had no heart to talk after that. He followed a path evidently so familiar that even though his eyes were open, he was trusting his feet alone. His eyes were in shadow, but the moonlight reflected on them darkly, so that I knew they were opened wide, staring at something beyond me, beyond what I saw.

I did not mind. I was heartened to see him wrapped up in his thoughts, which, though perhaps spurred by my presence, had little to do with me. I examined him more closely. He was compactly built, and his undyed wool clothes cut close to lean and muscular limbs. His skin was pale, almost to transparency, and his ears arched up at the tips. Despite a red scattering of pimples over his cheeks, in the dark he struck me as somewhat like the unicorns in his ability to catch the moonlight.

I thought again of Mrs. Helder's stories of the Old Folk. It was strange that Torun knew Gersan, but I had never heard such sounds as made his language since...since that mysterious girl with the lamb. And where was he leading me? Having an uncle was an accident of birth, not a guarantee of Torun's character. But what about Bettina? She sounded irretrievably lost, if not dead. Could the Old Folk die? He caught me watching him, and I quickly turned my face to the path ahead of us. But my eyes kept turning towards him. Yes, he looked weary with life.

"Not far now." He pointed ahead to a densely wooded area high above and across the wide, flat streambed we had reached. "There."

I saw nothing.

He jumped down into the riverbed and held out his hand to me. Perhaps this was part of a creature's trick, I wondered. No young man had ever performed such a gesture of courtesy for my benefit, and now Torun had done it twice. I stared, feeling blood rush to my cheeks. He dropped his hand and stepped back.

"My apologies. I forget, for a moment."

Torun had evidently much experience with leaping down from the rocks, but I sat down and slid myself ungracefully down to join him in the riverbed. Large, snow-covered stones were gradually replaced with smaller, flatter ones as we neared the stream.

He waded through and paused, calf deep.

"The river can be..." He raised his staff and hand and waved them about. He was trying to convey some meaning. Had Sida not been lost, I would have laughed to see the absolute break between the comedy of his arms and the solemnity of his face. Instead, I stared, uncomprehending.

"Ah...You need help?" He held out his arms, as if to mean he would carry me.

My face was burning. "No." My boots were thick and well-greased, and I splashed through to him. The current pressed the leather against my legs. "I'm just tired."

Within a few minutes it was almost completely dark.

"Not far." We scrambled up the other side of the bank and across a stretch of tall, dry grass to what seemed to be a thick hedge. We pushed through the bushes, which opened onto a small sloping clearing vaguely dotted with sleeping sheep. The bushes seemed to form a natural fence around their small pasture. In the middle of the pasture was a stout, gnarled, spreading oak tree. Built into the branches, supported by beams six feet high, was a clever little house with a portico that spanned the oak's largest branches.

Torun leaned his staff against the oak's trunk and called up in his language. The phrases seemed to begin with a stress and flow on in a monotone before lilting sharply up and down at the end.

Someone called back down, and a trapdoor opened in the portico floor. I blinked at the glow of firelight that spilled from the door of the treehouse. A ladder slid down to the ground.

Putting his palm upwards and bending his fingers towards himself, Torun gestured at me to approach, still speaking his language. I came to the ladder.

He pointed up. "You go." As I wearily pulled myself up the rungs, he added, "When he sees you, I wonder what my uncle will say."

When I reached the top of the ladder, a woman a few years younger than Ma, as pale and high-cheeked as Torun, was waiting for me with outstretched arms. I began to clamber onto the portico and she impatiently stepped forward, hooked her hands under my armpits and hauled me up through to the threshold. Torun was soon behind me, pulling up the ladder in easy, practised motions and closing the trapdoor. Inside, children's high voices called to Torun. He held the door open and responded rapidly, reassuringly to the children as the woman led me into the house.

The inside of the house was bright from a small fire in a domed clay furnace. As the light caught my face, the children's questioning voices fell silent.

"*Lavog?*" Torun said wearily, presenting me to four faces ranging from the beaky proportions of early adolescence to the rounded chin of early childhood. "*Bettina, ni Bettina.*" The smallest one, a little girl, ran to me, wrapped her fat arms around my legs and burst into tears.

The woman crouched, put her arms around the little girl's plump body and gently tried to pry her hands away, crooning "*Chuuu, chuuuu. Ni Bettina. Chuuu,*" in a voice thick with tears. The child clung harder.

"I'm sorry," I said. The harsh tones of my own language sounded louder in the tight space. The small child looked up at me in terror at the sound, released my leg and buried herself in her mother's embrace. In the moment that her face had been turned to mine, I saw with shock that she was different from the other children. The others were like Torun and the woman. Pale hair, pale angular faces, eyes like narrow triangles. The little one had fat, red cheeks and had thick, curly dark hair. Like mine. She could have been my sister. *She took the form she thought you might trust most*, I remembered Mrs. Helder saying.

I looked from the child to the woman to Torun, utterly failing to understand the web of connections. And like my small copy, I was beginning to feel my emotion overwhelm me, like a flood threatening a small island. My fawn, my Sida, was lost. I was lost. I had become a dead girl's ghost and my mother was far away. I gave a wet sniff. "I'm-m s-sor-ry."

Torun and the woman exchanged alarmed glances. She rose with the child balanced on one hip and gathered me to her and, though I was taller than she was, she brought my head to her shoulder. "*Chuuu*," she murmured, patting my hair, "*Chuuu*."

Meanwhile, Torun explained further to her and she nodded or shook her head in response. Finally, he paused, and I could almost hear him preparing to bend his tongue to my language.

"My uncle is in the village. He will return. You will stay."

I nodded, but kept my eyes closed and my cheek rested on the woman's shoulder. She smelled like wood smoke, with a comforting undertone of milk and dirty laundry. But then the door opened, and the trapdoor scraped across the floor. I opened my eyes and straightened.

"Torun!"

He froze, perched over the trapdoor. I felt a prickle across my skin as I realized that the entire family was listening. Hearing his name from my throat felt too familiar, too foreign, for them.

"Where are you going? Don't you live here?" He was the only one who spoke my tongue, the only one who knew where I had left my trail.

"No. Too many." And he swung out without even bothering to use the ladder.

Without Torun to talk to, I remained silent, reduced to gestures.

"Melina," the woman said, pressing her tapered fingers to her chest in a motion identical to Torun's. She sat me down and fed me smoked mutton stewed with beans. And watched me. Melina's lips lifted in a bittersweet memory when I unconsciously shared a gesture with her missing daughter or turned down when I tore my bread in a manner learned from my mother.

In turn, I observed her and her children in their odd home. It was a small room with different nooks and alcoves as the house followed the shape of the wide oak tree. One alcove had a big bed and another a narrow one, both half-hidden by thick curtains. In the largest alcove was a great loom and beside it, two spinning wheels and an assortment of smaller looms that could be held in a woman's lap. There were sacks of millet and barley meal stored here and there and sausages hanging from the rafters. At least they have sausages, I thought wearily.

Although the older children remained wary of me, the little one soon forgot my strangeness, especially when Melina pulled out a knee-length white shift for me to change into. All the children were already dressed for bed, but she sent the eldest with the two boys out to wash dishes while I rinsed my face and upper body in a bucket. The youngest child watched me carefully as I changed out of my dirty shirt, breeches and boots and pulled on the shift. Melina gave me a comb and then collected my clothes. When I tried to protest, she pointed her chin towards the child and then to the wide bed. The children all slept in one bed, and I, it seemed, would sleep with them.

After I had braided my hair, the smallest child, my miniature, came to me. I opened my arms and lifted her up. I had never held a child before, but this one clung to me like bony, dense ivy. With one small hand furled in the shoulder of my shift, she pointed to the rightmost edge. I sat down and pulled us over to the required spot. I felt her small body loosen and mold to mine.

"*Chuuu*," I said, wondering at how easily I was trusted.

The little child agreed. "*Chuuu*," she said, as the other children approached the bed.

Before they all climbed in, Melina named and kissed them each in turn.

"Sarai," was the eldest, a girl of about thirteen with freckles.

"Maro," a plump boy of ten-ish whose eyes tilted up at the tips.

"Dan," a boy a year or two younger, who shared the curl of his whitish hair with his youngest sibling.

Last of all, Melina kissed the littlest one on the crown of her brown head. "Telka." It was a show, I saw, to introduce us. Then she stepped away from the bed and pulled the dark blue curtain closed.

Although we two were cozy, I was aware of the gap of mattress between me and the next child. The older children whispered to each other in the dark but fell asleep one by one. I had never slept with another human except my mother, much less four strange children. These particular four kicked and mumbled in their sleep and stole the blankets. Telka sprawled across my chest. She twitched and drooled a little. At some point close to dawn, she rolled off me and burrowed into Dan. I drifted into sleep, thinking about my fawn, listening first to Telka's steady breathing and then to Melina, somewhere beyond the curtain, biting back tears.

I woke from a dream of someone whistling a song from long ago, one that was made to keep us awake as the pony cart rumbled down the country road. I realized I was sweating from the heat of five bodies in a small space and opened my eyes. Morning light frayed the edges of the curtain. The rumble and the song echoed in my mind as I looked over at Melina's children. How strange they must find me. How frightening. Had I been one of them, I would not want a ghost in my bed. I crawled out and saw that Melina had laid out a measure of stiff cloth the width of my arm and twice as long. Over the shift she had given me the night before, I wrapped the cloth around my middle like a skirt and, pulling it tight, tucked one end in. I slid past the curtain and into the main room.

And there he was.

Full beard. Curly, tousled hair fading from chestnut brown to grey. Round, low cheeks. Carving the peel off an apple into a long, scarlet spiral as he crouched on a stool by the embers of last night's fire in the small clay furnace. Whistling low, sweet and true.

I swallowed and found my voice before he could look up. I crossed my arms and said, "Hello, Pa."

CHAPTER SEVEN

Someone's Home

He laughed.

I might have flinched, but he did not seem to notice. The rumble from my dream still echoed in my ears and I almost missed his first words to me.

"Gods above, you've found me at last!" My father set down the apple and knife, stood up and embraced me. It was a quick, hard squeeze and release. He grabbed my shoulders and looked at me from an arm's length, giving me a little shake with each sentence. "I can see how poor Torun made the mistake. Melina told me. Damned close resemblance. You're mine, no mistake, hey little Beth."

"No one's called me Beth for years." Never, in fact. Had *he* called me Beth? I could not remember.

"Of course not. Elizabeth?"

I nodded. I felt numb, too surprised to feel outrage. All those years, I thought. After all those years pining after his memory, all I had to do was walk in a straight line across the forest.

"How did you find me? How shall we escape?" He seemed to sag down, tightening his grip on my shoulders. "Take me home to Sylvia!"

"What?" How could he joke about Ma when she had been through so much?

He laughed again. "I jest. There *is* no way of going home. Not for me. Now tell me sweet Elizabeth, how did you find your old Pa?"

As if I had been searching for him. As if it had been my duty to track him down. And hadn't I searched and yearned for him? I didn't know what to feel. "I wasn't looking for you. I was chasing after one of our animals. But we did wait for you."

"What do you mean? You can't have stayed at that dingy little meadow..." He laughed again. "Did Sylvia go back to her folk?"

"Victor gave us up long ago." I fought off a sneer. "We don't need his charity, anyway."

"But what have you lived on?" As if Ma wasn't wily enough to survive on her own...to call her helpless when *he* had left. No, Pa did not deserve the truth.

I thought of Sida and my voice caught. "Herding. Trading from our stock."

"Herding? I never could imagine Sylvia herding sheep. That's how we live here. Finest sheep I've ever seen. Wool like silk. Magical. The girls will show you. What do you herd?"

"Not sheep." I would not tell him, not after Julian. Unlike Julian, Pa was playful and jolly, but he was too ready to act like he loved me without earning my trust. What I had accepted in little Telka, I felt suspicious of in an adult.

"What then?" he asked keenly.

"Horses." I apologized silently to each of the unicorns. How indignant they would feel to be compared to domesticated animals who ploughed the fields and let brutish men and women ride them!

He snorted. "Sylvia's changed then. She never liked our pony."

I shrugged. "She has changed." And my heart gave a twist. What would she be like, had Pa stayed?

"But not you. You are as sweet as ever."

I could not return the compliment because I did not know him. Like Torun, he was wearing a shirt and trousers of fine, undyed white-grey wool. Above that, he wore an open vest that was leather on the outside and fleece on the inside. Underneath the vest, he wore a thick, red-bordered belt woven in a pattern of white rams in a green thicket. He was familiar as my flesh and so strange to my memory in dress and manner. He sensed my reserve and laughed again. Then, he pressed me onto a stool and began to make porridge.

I picked up the spiralled apple peel and nibbled on the end, thinking. Shocked and hurt as I felt, I couldn't help but sense that I must be careful in finding out the balance of power between me and him, between him and the others. After all, I only had one Pa, and he had many children. "How will you explain me to Melina?"

He threw up his hands, a wooden spoon in one of them. "She knows. Saw it as soon as you walked in. You're a little uncanny, one, and you're my daughter by another woman, two. You might be innocent in her eyes, but I am not. You've caused me an earful, sweet girl."

Melina? From what I saw of her the previous night, it must have been a quiet earful. I looked around. "Where is she now?"

"Leading the sheep out with Torun. To spare him the task of coming here. Don't be surprised if he's not eager to see you."

He seemed ready to say more but thought better of it. Instead, he ladled out porridge in a bowl for me and handed me a spoon. "Hmmm. Sylvia," he said meditatively, watching me.

I ate to avoid talking. I did not wish to speak of Ma to him. When he had known Ma, she had been someone very different from the woman I knew. His Sylvia had run away from a rich home to take up a life of romance and adventure; my Ma kept my life deliberately quiet.

He chuckled. "She fussed over you so."

Did she? I didn't want to ask. I didn't trust his memory.

Pa ladled out porridge for himself and took out a crock of honey. He drizzled some honey into his porridge and put the crock away before coming back to sit with me. I watched him. He was masterful. He did not leave space for a comment he did not want to hear, laughed off what should be barbs. He was absolutely content under my wary gaze. "It's strange how you are like us both. You and I both show our hearts on our faces."

I snorted.

"But you're moody like Sylvia." He made his assertions so bold that they attained the solidity of facts.

"Bettina?" Telka's sleepy voice emerged from the bed-nook. My father looked from me over to the curtain with raised brows.

"Bettina?" Her voice was louder.

I realized that he was not going to move from his seat. With a sigh, I crossed over and fetched the child from bed. Telka slipped her hand in mine and I led her out. When I sat down, she crawled into my lap and finished my porridge, while her father explained in her language that I was not Bettina, but Elizabeth.

"Lizbet," she said, accepting her father's words without surprise and gestured to me that I ought to wake the others.

"That was Bettina's job," my father said. "But..." he paused, with the barest hint of delicacy, "perhaps I ought to do it, today." He sauntered over to the curtain and knocked on the lintel. "Sarai, Maro, Dan." He knocked twice more and flung the curtain open. Maro was already crawling off the foot of the bed and bowled into his—our—father's middle. My—our—father ruffled his hair. Sarai rolled her eyes and looked over at Dan for solidarity, but Dan had already joined Maro and Pa. With a few short words from our father, the rest of the children understood that I was here to stay. Or at least, by the time they joined me at the table, Maro and Dan had already given me small smiles. Sarai curled her lip at me and then looked significantly at the

loom and spinning wheels. No one seemed curious about where
I had been found or how I had appeared. Or perhaps my father's
presence was enough to quell their curiosity. Not mine.

"Wait," I cut in. "Can't I go home?" I had eaten my father's
food and slept in his children's bed, but I did not belong in here
when Sida was somewhere out there, ranging through strange
hills. I needed to find Sida and get both of us home before
Ma returned from her journey. "Ma needs me." He ought to
know that.

Pa smiled. "Oh, Elizabeth, don't you want to stay here and
get to know your brother and sisters? What about me? I've
missed you so."

Four heads swivelled from me to Pa and back to me. Telka's
small hands pressed into my chest as she looked up at my
face. They didn't know our words, but they sensed the tension
between us.

I breathed in. I couldn't go home without Sida. Until I found
her, I would need a place to stay. "I should find yesterday's trail,
at least..."

He met my eyes. "But you can't," he said with a smile.

I was not smiling. He had not raised me, and he had no
power to command me. I stood up and set Telka down. I crossed
to the door and looked back deliberately.

"I can do what I want," I said. But when I flung open the
door, I saw that I was trapped. Not just by Pa, but by the turn
of the seasons.

It had not been warm in the home only because of the crowd
of human bodies. The rumble from my dream had not begun in
my head. Overnight, spring had arrived in a rage. Through the
sheets of rain, I could see that the flat riverbed that I had crossed
yesterday was roaring with thick, muddy meltwater, quickly dis-
solving sheets of snow, tangles of branches, a sodden clump that

looked like a drowned animal. I thought of Sida and felt a burning in my nose that promised tears. The landscape had been indistinct the night before, but now there was no possible way I could find my trail, let alone get back home. I looked up at the grey skies. They answered with a rolling crackle of thunder.

"Elizabeth, why don't you come and sit? Telka wants you."

I closed the door and sat down.

"The flood will last until late spring and it can rain for days," my father said. "You were lucky to arrive when you did."

"But, Ma…"

"There's nothing to be done, Elizabeth," he said, with just a trace of sympathy. He put his hand over mine and I was surprised that it felt warm and reassuring. I looked up at him. "I should have told you about the flooding. Why not take it as a gift? A gift to see another part of the world, to know your brothers' and sisters' love."

"But what can I do here?"

He released my hand and flung up his arms, as if in welcome. "What you can *do* is ladle out the rest of breakfast. Welcome to the family."

My mind was still caught on my mother conducting her travel and business as usual, on Mrs. Helder coming to visit and finding the house abandoned. I thought of Sida alone in a strange place. Could she have tried to cross the river? What if the flood caught her? I wouldn't find her in the treehouse. I needed to find a reason to get out, one that they would accept. "Can I help with the sheep?" I asked.

My father looked uneasy for a moment. "No. That's not a good idea." He did not have to say Torun's name.

"I don't have to be with the flock," I insisted. "I'm very good at foraging."

He cleared his throat and spoke over me. "In this house,

women have other work." He jerked his chin at the boys. "Maro. Dan." He stood, and the boys jumped and swung from Pa's arms. They squealed as he took striding steps out to the portico. I followed them to the door and looked out. Through the rain, I noticed a few bedraggled outbuildings in the tree- and shrub-lined enclosure, and in the north-east corner, another, much smaller treehouse. It was under this small outbuilding that the boys went with our father to split wood and who knows what else adoring boys do with their fathers on rainy days.

As for me, Telka's sticky fingers tugging on my wrist told me that I was going to have to plot my escape while I learned about the girls' industry. After we washed up using water from the overflowing rain barrels on the portico, Sarai directed me to the loom.

I stared at the wooden machine with utter incomprehension, at its broad, horizontal panel, the thick, wooden legs, the vertical contraptions, the infinity of threads.

"Lizbet!" Sarai patted the loom and then her skirt of stiff, dark blue. She took a step to the side and patted a small hand-loom that could easily fit between Telka's arms. Then she ran her long fingers along her waist. I understood that the large loom was for weaving the lengths of fabric that they wrapped around themselves as skirts and the small, narrow loom mounted on a board the length of my forearm was for creating the intricately patterned belts that they used to cinch women's skirts together or to break the grey-white of the men's clothes. Sarai's belt was red with white pinwheels and Telka's was white with a simple yellow stripe and a little red bird on each end. Last night, Melina's belt had been indigo blue with geometric red and white peacocks. I, for the moment, was beltless, though I suppose if I had to have one, I would have wished it to be dark green with Sida dancing across it. I understood that if my father had his way, I would soon be working their trade as well as wearing their clothing.

I shook my head and pointed to the doorway.

"*Pffft*." Sarai said, a sound that clearly translated to "keep dreaming."

"Please?" I said, hoping that my tone would be as transparent as hers.

"Pa," she said, in addition to some other words I could not catch. She disgustedly directed me to the spinning wheel.

Outside of braiding small and ugly carpets out of fraying unicorn velvet, I had no experience with handicrafts. I looked over to where Telka was busy carding wool. Obviously, she and Sarai and Bettina had been trained to this work. I had been trained to be outside with my heels sinking into the soft earth. After watching me poking around the wheel and hesitantly pushing on the pedal, Sarai heaved a world-weary groan and sent me to card wool with Telka. If Sarai had anything to do with it, I would be outside in the rain in an instant. But while my father was outside, I was staying inside.

Sarai took her place at the loom and began weaving the shuttle back and forth with great skill and precision, every so often sharing knowing looks with Telka, who kept changing my grip on the toothed paddles.

As I worked, I thought through my options. The rain would wash away Sida's tracks, but when the rain ended, the mud would catch the impress of her cloven hooves. Hopefully, Sida would have found high ground. High ground. I remembered that Torun and the sheep were in the high pasture. At home, Sida had treated our goats with curious disdain—what would she think of sheep? I wondered whether I should tell Torun about her. I wondered what his face would look like if I told him. Would his sadness lift or his eyes open with wonder, like Mrs. Helder's did when I told her of does and bucks and fawns? I tried to picture his face, an absurd thought; it had been so dark when I met him that I wasn't even sure of the colour of his eyes.

My hand slipped, and I dropped one of the carding brushes. Telka and Sarai sighed in unison.

By the time Melina returned, Telka had graduated from correcting my grip to smacking my hands and saying, "*Zasto! Zasto, Lizbet!*"

Melina removed her thick felt coat slowly and hung it by the furnace to dry. When she approached me, the woman's eyes were rimmed with pink as though she had been crying. Whereas Ma chased me out of her workshop whenever I interrupted her experiments, Melina simply watched. Then she sat by my side and wordlessly showed me how to brush the clumps of the wool until the fibres all pointed in the same direction and then how to tease this wool rolag from the hooked teeth. She then sat me down by the large loom. Perhaps if she and Sarai had been working on a solid colour, I might have understood, but the pattern of large and small arrowheads in crimson, black and white required a system of counting that I could not follow. Within two passes of the shuttle over the warp, I had spoiled the pattern and tangled the shuttles. My incompetence seemed to calm her, because I was not her daughter reformed, just a part of my father's inferior past.

That night, I could not sleep, and I did not want to. Yesterday, I had been bone-tired and distraught. I was still distraught, and after a day cooped inside, I was itching for fresh air. Beside me, Telka graduated to only clinging to my arm. The smell of seven bodies, of food, of wet woolen clothing, was overwhelming.

I waited for the children to fall asleep, for Melina's and my father's voices to fade away. I waited until I sure that they had turned in for the evening. My boots were under the bed, and I carried them in one arm. There was the patter of water on the roof, but trees always scattered water after the sky had closed. If the rain had stopped, the ground might dry overnight and I could start looking for Sida. If she had crossed the river, I hoped she hadn't gone far. I slipped out of the alcove and found my father with his face to the fire burning low in the clay furnace and his feet on the earthenware ledge. An unlit pipe lay in his right hand. He was asleep, most likely. I walked to the door quickly and quietly. But as I opened it, the wood creaked.

"Where do you think you're going?" my father asked in a low, measured voice. The very controlled quality marked him as either nervous or angry.

"Outside." My voice was louder than I had expected.

He jerked his head to the door. Outside, we could speak louder. Fine. That's where I wanted to be, anyway. The delicious, wet smell of spring air cut through the thick warmth of the house. We stepped out onto the portico. It was now spitting rain. The air was damp and cool. Poor Sida. Poor Torun, wherever he was. I pulled on my boots.

He didn't stop me, but said, "You can't run off in the night. Not you, especially."

At home, I obeyed Ma because I trusted her. With Pa, I hesitated. I didn't trust him, but I had no one else. I couldn't rebel if I did not understand.

"Please," he said. "Not before morning..."

I sat down with my back against the side of the house and my elbows on my knees. I thought I had an idea that something had happened to Bettina in the nighttime. But whatever it was, it wasn't something I could ask about. Not yet. Not if I wanted the truth.

"I'm not running off," I said. "It's too...I'm not used to so many people." I was surprised by my own honesty. "I can't sleep with all the...the *breathing* on me."

He nodded. "There are rather a lot of them. That's why I keep on trading."

"To leave them?"

"No, so I keep coming back to them."

I made an involuntary "chuh" of disgust, but he talked over me.

"You see, Elizabeth, I'm a simple man. I like to be admired by my family and I don't like to get involved in their petty sorrows. So, I stay home just enough so they don't find out how shallow I am."

I thought over this a little. Such a strategy would work very well for a charming tinker travelling from place to place, but it wouldn't have fooled Ma in our cramped pony cart. "Then, why are you being so honest with me?"

He winked at me. "Well, you're not very real to me yet, are you?"

I shook my head. Unbelievable. And, therefore, probably true. Part of me wished that Ma had taken Victor's offer. Pa wasn't worth mourning. I'd tell her so. But for now, I had to learn enough about Pa's life here to survive until the spring flood died down.

"Why hasn't Torun come home?" Torun's presence lingered in the house, although he stayed away. All through the day, his name flashed through my dark, muddled attempts to understand. I wanted to talk to Torun, but the thought of his return made me want to run, fast and hard. It also made my mind rush to form questions that I wanted to ask of him, questions I could never ask Pa.

My father shrugged. "The water's high and driving a wet, unhappy flock of sheep is no man's idea of a game. But he could come back, if he wanted." He did not seem too concerned.

I was relieved by his answer, irritated by his nonchalance. "Why did you teach him Gersan?"

He laughed "I taught Torun so I would have someone to talk to. I also taught Bett...my eldest girl, so Torun would have someone to talk to and practise with when I was gone. I thought he would help me trade when he reached manhood. Speaking Gersan would let us talk about the wares without the customers hearing. A steady partner is worth his weight in gold. Torun's not born to buy and sell, but he liked seeing and hearing more of the world. We did a few trips together from the time he was Sarai's age, until last winter."

"Who took care of the flock?"

"My eldest girl, when he was away."

My mind went to the ghost elf-girl I had met as a child. She had had a lamb. She had spoken Gersan. But she had been almost grown when I was still very small. Perhaps the creature I had met had also haunted Bettina? My line of thought was broken by Pa briskly continuing.

"The sheep would stay around the house, though. She's... she was...too good a weaver to waste." He avoided saying her name, which would have attracted his family's attention if they happened to drift in and out of sleep. "He was going to marry my...her, see? A year or two from now. The two of them made some pact before she had lost her milk teeth. He took her rather seriously."

"He would marry his cousin? Isn't Melina his aunt?" It happened sometimes at the Helders' village, but I still thought it strange.

"No, not quite so close. She's his second cousin, I think, but she raised him. Old enough to be his aunt. So."

"How old was Bettina?" My skin prickled. Torun, somewhere around my age, would be too old for a daughter of Pa's. "She was almost sixteen last year, when it happened."

Impossible.

She would have been seventeen now. But *I* was seventeen. I stared at him.

If he seemed uneasy about something, his was an everyday, natural unease.

"How..." I started, trying to understand what was absolutely *unnatural*. How could he have two seventeen-year-old daughters? Instead, I stuttered, "How long after you left us did...did... Where did you go after you left us?"

He shrugged and tapped his pipe on the railing. "The pony threw me and ran off. Hit my head and woke up with a fever. I wandered about in the forest. Somehow, I ended up here, with Melina leaning over me and nursing me."

"How long before Bettina was born?"

He took his time answering. His manner was easy, but I hoped his blood had the decency to rise a little in his cheeks. "Bettina came about a year in."

I felt heartsick. By any logical system of counting, Bettina should be just entering maidenhood.

He laughed at my expression. "You're such an innocent."

He made it sound like an insult, but I barely felt the sting. He was too foolish or too forgetful to notice that I should not be so close in age and appearance to Bettina. *What has happened? I thought, looking at him. To you, to me, to Bettina?* I longed to ask, but he continued before I could say another word.

"It was a waste to train Torun," he said, steering us back into safe territory. "Now when I'm in town, I have that scoundrel Heino," he said. He scratched his beard. "Elizabeth, I'm going to show you what a trusting old Pa you have and leave you out here by yourself." He nodded towards the house, where the others slept. "But you have to come back inside before the others wake up in the morning. Especially Telka. You don't know what it would look like to them."

He went inside, and I lay down on the portico and stretched myself out across the worn boards.

Unreal, I thought with the beat of my heart. Unreal. Impossible.

And yet, Mrs. Helder had told me stories of young people wandering out of the forest for a night and coming out to find their grandchildren were grown. And now, somehow, I—like my father before me—had found myself on the other side of something, something that was in the Fenlen Forest or *was* the Fenlen Forest.

How could I ever find my way home now? Ma would find herself utterly alone. If I went back, would I find her and the Helders long dead?

And yet, the Fenlen Forest had been my home for many years. The forest had never hurt me or cut me away from myself in the way it did now. I grasped onto that fact. If I had somehow wandered out of sync from my life, had Sida come with me? She must be with me. I had to see if she was here. And then I would return to Ma through Fenlen Forest. Somehow.

The rain came harder now. Raindrops smacked hard against the wood and shattered into a fine mist. I shivered. I would have to wait until the rain stopped and simply be my father's daughter for a while. Simply! With what I knew, how could anything be simple?

Could I have seen Bettina, so many years before? How? Why? I couldn't believe it. Or else...

When I was small, Mrs. Helder had been concerned about the girl with the lamb stealing my shape. On winter nights, she had told me about children who were lured away by the Old Folk and the strange creatures who took their place. Changelings.

I wondered if I had accidentally become one.

CHAPTER EIGHT

A Change in the Weather

It's easier to deny that something strange has happened when you can't say anything about it. I was silent, and during the incessant rain of the next six days, the disturbing fact that time had somehow slipped its chain in the Fenlen Forest fell into the back of my mind. It didn't change anything, really. I still had to do the same things—find Sida, get home. I just didn't know what would be waiting for me there.

I made my escape from the house a week later, when the bad weather broke. Every morning I had looked out from the portico with less and less hope of finding my way back. The rain had grown stronger and then weakened in turns without stopping. The river swelled above its banks, and I understood why we lived in a treehouse and why Torun had led the sheep away. His absence meant a week of Melina's tortured attempt to explain the loom in words I did not understand. I lived in a lonely silence. After finding me still in the treehouse the next morning, Pa decided that honesty was not, after all, the best policy. He was playful, slick and evasive. Without anyone but Pa to speak with in my native Gersan, the sounds of their tongue and the shape of their lilting words began to flicker through my dreams. I became uneasily aware that, but for my father, I might start to forget my mother's language.

And then, the clouds finally scudded west across the river and towards the forest. The tepid sun revealed a sludgy landscape.

The watery morning light cast itself over the puddles and rain-drops that trembled on each leaf and beaded each strand of grass. Dressed in my breeches, I hauled up the trapdoor and let it fall to the wooden boards of the portico floor with a damp thud. I was feeding the ladder through the floor when I heard the pat-pat-pat of Telka's bare feet. She threw open the door, panting a little. I did not want her to be scared or cry at the sight of me running off—there was no guarantee I would find Sida, and if I didn't, I would still need to come back to my father's house to sleep and eat.

"*Ni zafor!*" I whispered gleefully as the ladder hit the ground with a squelch. "No" and "rain" were two of my recently acquired words. Telka was my main source of vocabulary. She was proud of teaching me, since I spoke like a child a few years younger than her. I gave a small whoop of happiness that Telka echoed back to me. As I pulled on my boots, Telka ran back to look inside and put a finger to her lips. They were still sleeping. Excellent. I waved at her and started climbing down.

The earth was saturated, and when I stepped down, muddy water came up almost to my booted ankles. Telka, barefoot in her nightgown, was already halfway down the ladder. When I was her age, Ma's worst fits of exasperation came when she was frustrated and tired after a day of work only to see me come home filthy. I imagined that a morning scrub would not please Melina. I turned and patted my shoulders and waist.

Telka, being the youngest of a large family, instinctively climbed onto my back. I anchored her legs with my arms and I stepped out into the early morning sunlight. I had not set my boots to the ground in over a week and before this morning, my eyes had always been trained on what lay beyond the yard—the river, the hills. Although I had only seen the hedged meadow on the night of my arrival, I now saw that within this meadow were two three-walled shelters—a summer kitchen with its own clay furnace in the southeast corner and a larger shed for the sheep inside a pen in the northwest corner. Beside the pen was a henhouse, from which the disgruntled clucking of damp, cooped birds came. Now I understood what Dan and Maro and Pa had been doing throughout the week. The poultry had needed feeding, and the sheep shelter had been re-shingled and filled with clean hay. From the ground, I saw that there were cisterns to catch rainwater above each building. Along the northeast side of the yard was a fenced off, muddy vegetable garden within which stood a shed on stilts that I supposed held extra supplies.

Telka nudged me with her heels and I made a neighing sound like a horse. She laughed, pulling on the neck of my shirt with one hand. She wanted to go out of the little confine of the yard, and so did I. Telka pointed me towards the narrow, crooked gap in the hedge and we were free in the great world.

The rain had beat away the chill of winter, and the tall grass leading down to the swollen river smelled green and new. I couldn't set out and find Sida with Telka wrapped around me, but looking out across the river helped me think about how I might try next.

From up the hill, we heard the distant sound of bells and the bleating of sheep on the move.

"*Torun!*" Telka said, kicking my thighs.

I looked up. He was busy minding the flock, and I could inspect him without catching his gaze. Though lean, he was not as tall as I remembered, but he seemed more solid with his face and clothing speckled with mud. His movements were easy and loose as he jostled and was jostled by the sheep. His eyes were narrow shadows that contrasted with his sunlit hair, the strong lines of his cheeks and nose and chin. Looking at him, I felt the knot of unease loosen slightly in my chest. He looked at peace.

Until he saw me.

Telka shrieked his name again. "Torun! *Hin-ye!*"

"Where you take Telka?" he called, a note of panic in his voice.

Telka laughed and shouted something. I started walking up the hill towards him. When I was three steps away, he paused midstride. One of his dogs—they were both grey with fur that curled like the sheep's—ran up to him, curious at the change in pace. Torun crouched down to ruffle the animal's head before whistling an order. The dog wheeled around the edge of the herd, but Torun stayed there a moment longer before straightening and meeting my gaze.

I stopped where I was. I felt my face grow hot, felt the hair on my arms prickle.

"Hello," he said.

"Hello, Torun." *Run*, my skin said. *No*, my feet replied, *stay*.

Torun's half-smile suggested that he sensed my embarrassment and shared it.

"You missed home?" I asked, all too aware of Telka watching us.

He didn't answer for a moment. "Some sheep…how do you say …*utta*…woman-sheep?"

I dredged my memory for the word. "Ewe?"

"Some of my…ewes…will have lambs…*voon*. Now that the rain ended, it is more safe here."

Telka, gripping my waist with her legs, stretched her arms out to him, a gesture leftover from babyhood. He stepped close to me, and his hands brushed my shoulder as he lifted her from my back. We were both careful not to acknowledge the touch by any glance or shift in our bodies. He balanced her on his right hip, and she looked up at him in admiration. He kissed the top of her head "Until the ewes and *voon* are strong, it is practice for Maro and Dan."

"*Voon?*" Telka cried, now struggling to get down from her perch. He set her down and she began squelching through the mud, passing her hands over the sheep and looking for the heavily pregnant ewes. "*Voon?*"

"Telka, *ti mi voon vog,*" he called to her. She grinned at him with a streaky, muddy face. So much for keeping Telka clean. But now that she wasn't in my arms and Torun was watching her, perhaps this was the moment.

"Torun?" I began, and he looked up at me sharply. His eyes were a dark brown, the colour of rich loam.

"Torun, I..." How did you explain that your rebellious unicorn fawn was lost, probably wounded, perhaps caught in some other moment of time altogether? It sounded so unreal...

"Torun! Telka! Lizbet!" It was Sarai, calling from the portico. Although the timbre of her voice was brighter than her mother's, she had already developed a tone of command. I didn't need to understand her words to know that Telka was in trouble for being dirty and I for letting her run in the mud.

Torun called back to her and began herding the sheep down to the hedge.

"You will not be in so much trouble," he said. The left edge of his mouth lifted fractionally. "I explain you to Sarai."

"That's very brave of you."

He nodded. "Yes," he said, walking ahead of me to grab Telka's hand and lead the flock.

I smiled at his willingness to admit that a person needed bravery to face Sarai. A week with her had taught me that she was the true taskmaster of the weaving operation. If Melina's belts were more intricate, it was only because she had more experience. But where Melina had ample patience, Sarai had none. Sarai respected skill and nothing else.

As we chased the last sheep through the hedge, I saw that I was not the only one anxious to leave the house. Up on the portico, Pa was packing up his wife's and daughters' woolen wares. He was heading out on a trading trip, it seemed. Fine, I thought. My life wouldn't be that different without him. It wasn't as if I would miss any soul-searching conversations.

As he rolled the materials, Sarai stood above him with her arms crossed, unfolding them every few seconds to count off on her fingers before refolding them in a show of firmness. Fixing prices, I guessed.

As I passed through the hedge, Maro and Dan were scrambling down the ladder to meet the flock. Torun grinned easily as he met the children. He joked with Maro and gave Dan a piggyback ride. Sarai hung back, too old for roughhousing, young enough to pout with jealousy. She glared at me as I climbed the ladder.

I smiled and nodded at her. At this moment, I did not need to please her. Then I pulled myself up and addressed my father.

"Can I write a letter to Ma?" I asked.

"With what, child?" my father said.

"I'll write to her, and you'll send it on at the next town. You'll have to give me a quill and pen."

"No. I don't have any."

"What do you mean?" I thought of my mother's meticulous business ledgers and her diary of experiments. "How else do you do your business?"

He lifted his arm and pointed to what seemed like a half-finished bracelet of different coloured threads. "With this. I keep track of sales and things. Your mother was the one who could write, not me."

"But…" But Ma would be due home soon. What would Mrs. Helder tell her? Where would Ma go to look for me? And then I remembered. Even if I wrote a letter and Pa sent it, I had no way of knowing that Ma would receive it. Perhaps she had come home years ago. Perhaps she had already died and turned into grave dirt.

My father saw the flush on my face and put a hand on my shoulder. "I will see what I can do, Elizabeth. Leave it to me."

How could I trust my first betrayer? With the river rushing at my back, I had no other choice.

By noon, he had walked away from us into the eastern forest, whistling his favourite song. His family had changed, his business had changed, but he remained disconcertingly the same.

In his absence, his family seemed to stretch and shift. Sarai was the undisputed mistress of the loom, and Melina and Torun ran the farm. After Melina had me change into a shift and skirt, we sorted the twenty pregnant ewes out of the flock and led them into what I understood to be the lambing pen. Then we sat in the hay and listened to Torun's explanations as he inspected each of his "women-sheep," silently waiting for the lambs to come.

In the late afternoon, Melina summoned me and Sarai to help prepare the evening meal. We brought everything—the plates, spoons and stew—down so that we could eat with him. We sat with him late into the night, them conversing in hushed voices, me listening hard for any words I understood.

Right as Melina announced that it was time for bed, Torun announced that he had carved them something special over the week. He teased them, reaching into his bag and then refusing to reveal it.

"*Zasto* Torun!" Telka shrieked before we hushed her. Bad Torun, I understood. For example, Telka had taught me that my carding and spinning and weaving was very, very *zasto*. *Zastola*, in fact.

Torun laughed and slowly drew forth a small wooden figure. My gasp matched those of the children and Torun glanced at me, still smiling. The carving had delicate cloven hooves, grooves to indicate the downy fur, a delicate, spiralling horn.

"*Uksarv,*" Telka said. Unicorn.

"She's perfect," I said.

"Almost," he said. "I made the..." with his finger he drew a horn in front of his head, "longer, so the children would understand."

"Yes," I said. I wanted desperately to stay with him when the others went. I wanted to settle into the hay and ask him how and when and perhaps even why he had seen a unicorn. It had to be Sida, I thought. It *must* be.

I held his gaze, hoping that he might read in my face the longing and determination to see what he had seen.

Before he could nod or make any gesture of recognition, Telka bowled into him, giving him a hug. She did not like us talking mysteries in front of her. He looked away, his cheeks pink.

There was a moment of quiet, and then Melina and Sarai began bustling. Sarai stacked the dishes into buckets for Maro and Dan to wash. Melina handed Telka into my arms. She placed a firm hand on the centre of my back to direct me towards the house and up the ladder.

I paused on the portico. I had planned on running straight back down to talk to Torun. Melina had become used to me sitting out in the evening. But not today. "*Ni,*" she said, with rare sternness.

I wasn't sure whether she was curtailing my freedom because of Pa's absence or Torun's presence. Instead of sending me to bed, she sat me down by a handloom and tapped the belt I had been working on. Over the past week, she had insisted that I unpick my belt pattern on the handloom three times. Now she wanted me to finish it and watched me as the others washed their faces and went to bed. The pattern was not a unicorn, as I would have liked. It was horizontal stripes of red and white, the simplest of designs.

Dan was snoring when Melina gave a nod of approval and produced her pocketknife to cut the ends. I knotted the threads together, three to a bunch. She tapped my shoulder to make me stand and wrapped it twice around my waist before tying it off. She stepped back and sighed. I had a belt tied around my waist and she had done her duty.

"*Naisik*," she said, cupping my face with her hand.

Another one of my few words. By making my own belt, I was no longer an unformed child.

I was a girl.

And, secretly, I was a girl who was going to find Sida.

CHAPTER NINE
Overgrowth

I went to bed, but I did not fall fully asleep. I drifted in and out of dreams that smelled like an autumn wind. When everyone else was asleep, I crept out into the main room in my shift and jacket. If I did not want Melina to know I was sneaking out, I had to keep my other clothing clean.

The moon was bright above the hedges. When I crept down the ladder, I found that while the hot sun dried the mud, the night air cooled it, made it moist. Around the yard, the sheep slept in huddled white lumps. The lambs and ewes were in their pen; Torun would be dozing there with Maro and Dan.

I wouldn't go far, I promised myself as I took a few steps forward. I just wanted to see the sky when I was not penned in by trees.

Beyond the hedge, the stretch of the heavens took my breath away. The stars lay thick and luminous against the dark. On the first nights I had been here, the clouds had blocked the sky. To go out would have been dangerous, especially in the shadows of the forest trees. But in the open, I could see the faint glow of the river, the silhouette of the forest, the tilt of the mountain on my right…and…there.

A shape that seemed to hold her own dim light, long legged, but still short bodied.

"Sida?"

She was a good distance from me, but if I stepped carefully and swiftly…

"Sida!"

She whickered, danced closer to me. Only a bit farther...

I tripped on a branch and fell face first into the dewy grass. As I picked myself up onto my hands and knees, I felt her hot breath in my hair. I knelt and looked up at the greyish blur that was her face. "I missed you," I said, touching her downy cheek. She snuffled at me while I stood and ran my hands down her neck and shoulder. My hand caught a groove, and my fingers felt hot and damp. Sida stepped quickly sideways. I had touched a deep scratch or a cut.

"Who's done this to you?" I said, though she could not answer. Staying outside alone now seemed stupid, unwise.

I thought of the safety of the hedge, where the sheep slept. I slipped my arm under her neck and entwined my fingers in her short mane.

"Come on, girl, let's get you somewhere safe." I stepped forward and gave the gentlest tug.

Sida whinnied and pulled back violently. I tripped backwards and fell hard on my seat.

I stood up and started running after her, but she swiftly disappeared into the dark of the forest. Only a fool would go there at night, without anything to light the path. I was left with a handful of short hairs from her mane, tinged with blood from her cut. I wiped my hands on the grass and rolled the hairs together into a wad, pocketing them.

Somehow, perhaps, they would lead me to her again.

With tears in my eyes, I made my way back to the hedge.

In the closer dark of home territory, I saw a small burst of sparks. Someone had stirred the fire outside the lambing pen. The flame flared up, and the red glow lit up the face of the person blowing it to life.

"Torun!" I said, walking forward carefully, eagerly. He would understand.

There was a thud, of someone falling backwards in surprise.

"*Ki-yen?*" he whispered hoarsely. Who's there? Of course, with his face to the fire, he would be blind to the sight of me coming through the dark.

"Torun, it's me!"

The fire flared higher now, and the light caught my hands and warmed my face as I climbed over the fence and into the lambing pen. In the flickering light, I could see Maro and Dan curled up like snails in their shells, fast asleep in the far corner of the shed.

"What...what are you doing outside? Now?" Torun's eyes were overshadowed by his brow and his mouth was strained. His tension was like that of a horse sensing a coming storm.

I paused, leaned my back against the rails of the fence. I had wanted to tell him about seeing Sida, but my sheer relief, my hope, my disappointment and my worry all paled against his fear. This was the second time he had called to me, thinking I was Bettina. Had he seen her on other dark nights like this? I shivered.

"I'm sorry...can I come a little closer to the fire?"

He looked at me a moment, exhaled in a slow, contemplative manner. He wasn't sure about me, I saw, but he still shifted a little to the right and extended his left arm as a gesture for me to come nearer. He then set his arm down to prop himself up more surely.

"I wanted to look around at night," I said as I came over. "And then I saw you..." When I sat, I had intended to leave some space between us, but the shadows were tricky and I landed snug against him, thigh to thigh. His shoulder touched the right edge of my back. I looked over to apologize and found our noses almost touching. I was so close I could tell he had been chewing spruce resin after the evening meal.

We fit together, and in the dark, this frightened us both. I slid away.

"I think I saw...ah, um...outside, by the river," I managed.

"You were outside?" Torun repeated, his voice hoarse.

"I..." I balked at telling the truth about Sida. It wasn't the right time. Torun was already scared, and if I told him I was with a unicorn, it might confirm his suspicions about me. "It's not fair," I burst out. "This is not fair! I am not supposed to be here! It's all wrong!" I had told a sort of truth, but in saying it aloud, I thought I might still sound suspicious.

Torun gave an odd, tense smile. "Do you miss home?" he asked.

It seemed an obvious question, but I did not know how to answer it. I wanted to be with Ma, before Julian's and Victor's last visit. "I wish I could go back," I said.

"Even with your father living here?"

"Pa?" The surprised tone of my voice was louder than I had wanted. I swallowed. "He left us. After seeing him again, I wonder why Melina would want him."

"Your father, Melina, they have a business as well as a family. No wool, your father starves. No selling...well, we cannot live on mutton alone. He is kind to the children. And Sarai, she is one he respects."

This was the most I had heard in my own language for what felt like years. He seemed to have thought the words many times. I realized that Torun did not trust Pa. I was surprised by a rush of fellow feeling.

"And you?"

Torun said nothing.

"Then why do you stay around? Why can't *you* sell the wool?"

"Who would watch the sheep? When I went to trade..." He paused. Bettina had tended the flock, Pa had said. "They are my blood. They have no one in the family who cares as much. I am here for them, for *her*."

For her. I shivered. "You're trapped?"

"No." His answer was firm. "*I* am not. It is my choice." He chewed on his thoughts a little. "We were going to marry. It was our plan. Go away to a new village. Start a home. And then Melina and the children could come and join us. Or the children."

"Whose plan was it?"

"Bettina. She saw early how the world worked. She was…" He tapped his temple with a finger. "She was keen."

"Couldn't you do it now?"

He shook his head. "I'm not close enough blood to have Sarai come and live with me. She's almost old enough to be married. People would talk."

"I like Bettina," I decided. Bettina had thought things through, I realized.

"I like Bettina also. She was my friend."

What happened to her? I wanted to ask. But after Pa's evasions, I felt reluctant to pry. I knew both too much and too little.

As we gazed out at the night, I silently wondered whether she would like me. "Am I like her?"

He laughed, a rich, full sound. "No. Yes. You look like her. You are not so gentle."

"That's not fair," I said indignantly. "Telka likes me!"

"You are gentle to those you think deserve it. Bettina was kind to all."

"Hmph." I thought kindness was overrated, except with unicorns.

He gave me a small push on the shoulder. "Don't be sad. Being too gentle is hard on the soul. It was hard for Bettina. It is good for me that you are not like her."

I put my hand down into the straw and I accidentally set it on his.

Torun leapt up.

I took my hand away and set it in my lap and held it with the other, as if to stop it from escaping and accidentally reaching for Torun again.

We stared at each other, neither one of us trusting one another or ourselves.

One of the boys stirred in the corner, and in some horror of being seen, I stood up fast and ran off towards the house, this time slipping between the rails of the pen, a less elegant, but swifter retreat.

Torun did not call after me.

I climbed up to the house in the tree and undressed clumsily before climbing into bed.

In the close darkness of the bed, I sniffed back tears. I had spooked Sida and now I had done the same—or worse—to Torun. I understood neither of them and I confused myself, too. A small hand patted me over my right eye and cheek.

"*Chuuu*," Telka murmured sleepily.

But Telka's sympathy would not put things right. It would not help me find Sida. For Sida, I needed Torun. I would have to make things right.

The next morning, I woke up early and climbed down the ladder with a pail of cold, stewed mutton sausage, fermented cabbage and onion.

The boys were splitting wood and Torun was in his shed. There was a small fire going outside the lambing pen, and orange embers glowed in a pit where he kept a cauldron of water hot. Beside the cauldron, there was a dish of sludgy soap and a bucket for washing his hands. Three new lambs waggled their tails as they drank milk from their mothers' teats. There was a faint, pink blush on their white fleece. Torun had scrubbed blood from under his fingernails during the night. I shuddered.

I would hand him his food and leave. No. I would hand him

his food and apologize. And then I would ask about Sida. What was the word for unicorn? I struggled and failed to find the right sounds. Perhaps I *should* just leave after I gave Torun the food. I felt my heart beating faster as I approached the lambing shed. I needed to escape the house. No. I *did* know my words. I had been practising them.

When he stood up and came towards me, I felt my tongue grow thick, shy, stupid. Torun looked at my tense face and sent the boys upstairs to start breakfast for the others.

He took the pail from my hands and nodded his thanks.

How could we speak after what had happened the night before?

I lost my nerve and I was half over the fence when one of the ewes lay down and began to pant heavily. For a moment, my foot stayed planted on the railing. I would stay. As I lowered myself back into the enclosure, her hooves raked at the soft earth as her legs twitched with each breath. Astounded, I watched as a transparent, gelid membrane emerged from under her tail.

"Ah," Torun said with satisfaction. "I have been waiting for this one." We waited together as the membrane swelled. Inside, distorted from the fluid, the hooves and then nose and then eyes and ears of a lamb appeared. The ewe heaved and slowly, slowly, the lamb inched further from her body.

"Shouldn't you help her?" My voice was shrill.

Torun shook his head and as the lamb's shoulders emerged, the rest of the body slithered out. The ewe stood up, and as she bit through the membrane and nuzzled her lamb, her sides began to heave again. The ewe kept attending her lamb as *another* pair of thin legs and small head coated in a yellow-white membrane slid from her. She turned around, barely surprised, and began to chew through the second membrane to allow the other lamb to breathe. She began licking its tiny wet face and stick-like hooves.

Satisfied, Torun nodded. "Shall we eat?"

"Bleugh!" I could not even imagine chewing mutton sausage. Meat squeezed though a membrane...hot and damp like a fresh-born lamb.

"Bleugh?" Torun asked as we walked to the shelter. "What is *bleugh*? It does not sound like you are congratulating her."

Congratulations were the last thing on my mind. Birth was horrific—the mother's strained breath and the phlegmy, gelatinous sac that covered the lambs made me clench my teeth with the effort not to gag. "I was just surprised."

"You have never seen one of your animals give birth?" Torun asked.

"No! Well..." I had never seen *anything* give birth. Ma always chased me away when our nanny goat dropped her kids and the Helders' housecat hid herself away when she had kittens. "Our animals are more...private."

"But they still do it," he said with a half-smile, the benign echo of Sarai's sneers.

I told myself that it was impossible to imagine a doe-unicorn wheezing and rolling her eyes in exertion. But even as I thought it was impossible, I thought of Sida and the winsome ugliness of her first fawnhood. She was not unlike the lambs, perhaps.

I glanced over at Torun and found that he was watching me with his dark eyes. My face grew warm. He knew something of what I thought; he knew what I was feeling and though he smiled, he did not laugh. As we ate, I turned my attention to the lambs, whose spindly legs were spread in squat, bowlegged attempts to stand.

Although the first spoonfuls had been difficult to swallow, I regained my appetite and my determination. "Torun, I am sorry for yesterday. I scared you."

"I was not scared," he said lightly.

I let that pass. "I was hoping that I could help you herd."

"You?" His tone was not accusatory. "I could have Maro or Dan."

"I told my father that I herd at home." I ate more to avoid catching his eye.

"I know. Maro said." He glanced up at the house in the tree. Inside, Melina was laughing and she was joined by another light voice. Sarai, I realized with surprise. "You are a great help to them," he began slowly.

"I am not!"

"Not with weaving," he said with a quirk of his lips. "With other things. It is good for Telka…"

I could not let him say no. "I could help you practise Gersan. Please. I'm also terrible at carding wool. And spinning. And weaving." I gestured to my new belt. "This, *this*, took me *days*. Melina made me stay up late yesterday to finish it."

"That is because you did not wear a belt when you met me on the hill." He pursed his mouth and the tips of his ears flushed. He ran a hand quickly over his own belt, which was undyed wool with blocky black birds. "Melina did not like that. A person without a belt is…is…a person with no clothes."

"Having no belt is not like being *naked*!"

The corners of his eyes lifted as he smiled at my outrage, and then he looked down again. The sudden shyness made me aware that however I had been dressed yesterday, on the first night we met I had seen Torun in naked anguish, confusion, distress. I felt a strange rush of tenderness and I fought to find the words to express myself.

"I am a decent girl." That's what Mrs. Helder had always said about me and what Ma had wanted to make me, though it sounded stodgy.

He shrugged, his smile fading. "Now you are, but…decent…

girls do not herd sheep with strangers." He did not look at me as he scraped the spoon along the bottom of the pail.

It was time for the truth, then.

"I don't need to herd sheep, Torun...I need to go out to find my...my..." I found the word and started again. "Last night, I wasn't trying to run away. I saw my *uksarv*. But she ran away from me." Admitting Sida's rejection out loud made it so much worse.

"It is difficult to herd at night."

"I need to find her, and you saw her, so...I need your help. She's lost."

He tossed the spoon at the pail. It skimmed the rim and clattered to the bottom. "I know. But the forest is...it is big. Dark, too."

"I *can't* stay inside all the time. We can tell Melina I was tracking an animal...a horse...from my herd when you found me, and I think it is nearby." That was at least close to the truth.

"If you want to go so much..." He was silent for a moment and looked up again at the house nestled in the trees. "They do not own you, you know. I say it is good for you to stay, but you could just walk away."

"You saw her. I want you to show me where." That made sense and he couldn't deny it.

"You might not see a thing."

That was not a no. Which meant he was saying yes.

"Promise me, Torun?"

I felt rather than saw him glance at my face. But when I turned to look, he was watching the flock intently. The seconds stretched out. What had I said wrong?

"Go, go," Torun's voice was weary. "I will think and then come to talk with Melina." He squinted as one of the newborn lambs' legs gave way underneath it. "I promise."

I went upstairs. Melina and Sarai faced the fire, stirring the porridge. Maro, and Dan were stacking up the day's worth of firewood. Telka, sitting at the table, stared as I went straight to the bed and pulled my pack from underneath my spot on the bed.

Telka asked where I was going. "*Kurre*," I said. Out there. I crouched over my pack. Maro looked indignantly at his mother. If anyone was supposed to be with the sheep, it was him and Dan. It was their job. Dan let his brother speak for both of them. He didn't seem to mind being inside.

As Melina served the porridge, Sarai watched me warily. I unpacked. I wouldn't need my oil sheet or blanket, so I slid them back under the bed. The children stared at me. Melina pretended not to see. I took out my waterskin. I was nearly ready.

Torun came in just as I was going to the water barrel.

He leaned against the doorframe and murmured something to Melina, soft enough that the children could not hear. She strode over to him immediately and tugged the collar of his vest. That was her signal for him to follow her out to the portico. She closed the door behind him. This is what their conversation sounded like from our places at the table:

".."
".........Torun!..............."

That is to say, they spoke in whispers, only becoming audible in their moments of greatest frustration. As I was beginning to recognize snatches of everyday conversation, it seemed that Melina now wanted neither me nor the children to understand.

Finally, Melina burst out with, ".........*ni* Bettina, Torun!'"

A moment later, the door slammed open. The sun fringed Torun with light but made his core a dense shadow.

"Come on," he said. "We go now." He said something more to Maro and Dan in a brisk voice. Maro looked surprised and proud, Dan merely pleased. Responsibility over the flock, I supposed.

Melina continued to talk at Torun in a low voice while I gathered my things. I slung my pack over my shoulder, ready to go.

As I passed her, Melina grabbed me by the shoulders, holding my arms tight. Her face was chalky white.

"I'll be back," I said, "before the sun goes down."

Torun translated, flinging up his hands with exasperation. Then, to me, he said, "Come."

The pressure of her fingers eased. She stepped away and ducked her head down.

"Come," Torun repeated.

We walked out of the tidy perimeter of home without a word. We did not speak as we began the ascent beside the swollen river, breathing in the smell of meltwater and the muddy, tangled banks.

I looked around, scouring the landscape for a trace of Sida. It seemed all so ordinary. Trees, trees, rocks, leaves in the yellow-green of new growth, almost gold, red.

Red?

I stopped and looked across the river and up at the escarpment. There was a row of trees with leaves of fiery autumn orange and scarlet. I hadn't noticed that before...I felt a cool breeze on my cheek

Someone screamed, across the river. A girl. And then the sound of hooves. I stepped forward to see.

I blinked and when I opened my eyes again, I could not find the line of autumn trees again amongst the burgeoning green. And here, down by the river, the air was absolutely still. I would have felt the wind stir from a dragonfly's wings.

"Did you hear that?" I asked. "Did you see?"

"See what?" Torun said. He followed my pointing finger across the river.

"There...I heard something. And there were autumn trees..."

He frowned. "Where?"

But I could not show him. Had I imagined it? I squinted, trying to find a trace of colour or sound.

After a moment, Torun walked on. "Come. Your *uksarv* is not there."

I ran after him.

CHAPTER TEN
Wild Beasts

We turned away from the riverside and entered the forest. To my confusion, Torun seemed quite content to remain in silence. He walked beside me without looking at me. Perhaps my bodily presence was sufficient to capture—refracted—the privacy and intimacy he missed with Bettina. He whistled in answer to the larks and flycatchers and nuthatches. Rattled by the memory of the scream, I tried to pay attention to what was around me. The trees were different from the towering giants of Fenlen Forest. As we ascended, the elms and beech trees with budding, spreading branches gave way to the whispering green needles of spruces and pines. Now we heard different birds—the song of chaffinches, the pok-pok-pok of a lazy woodpecker. These trees, these birds, sounded different...*felt* different from the forest across the river.

I grew uneasy.

I had spent long summer days without human company, wandering in Fenlen Forest, but I would come home to chatter with Ma or Mrs. Helder at dusk. Now I had been barely communicating for more than a week. Torun was the only soul I could hope would understand me.

The path was steep here, but nothing that would have stopped a person from tossing a few comments to their companion. Yet he was silent. I wondered about his whispered battle with Melina. He had seen Sida and he knew she meant something to me. So why wouldn't he acknowledge me?

As the incline began to level off into a plateau, I thought of his silence another way. The conversation with Melina had forced him to remember that if he looked at me full on, rather than from the corner of his eye, he would not find Bettina looking back at him.

I gave a "chuh" of irritation at my own sentimentality. It quite ruined whatever spell he might have wished to cast from my presence, because he finally turned to me as we entered from the forest into the tall grass of the pasture.

"Yes?" he was almost smiling now.

I did not want to plunge him back into sadness and I had important business at hand.

"Is this where you saw Sida?"

"What is this word? Is it *uksarv* in Gersan? Is it one *uksarv* or many *uksarv*? For us, there is just one word."

I shook my head. "Sida is my *uksarv*," I explained. "She's been...mine...and special since she was very little."

I looked away, around at the field. It was larger than I expected, with just one tall, bare deciduous tree in the middle. The tall grass was empty. There was a small stream winding its way down the southeast edge that pooled for a little and meandered into the forest. All was quiet but for the rustle of wind kissing the grass and the tops of the trees and the occasional bright, sharp chirp of a meadow pipit.

"When did you see her?" My voice was quiet.

"The second day. When the sun was going down."

"Why? Why would she show herself to *you*?"

He seemed to fold into himself.

I thought of the first unicorn I ever saw, of my deep misery. Of feeling lost and abandoned. Oh, I knew why a unicorn would be drawn to him, why Sida would be curious and interested. I looked down at his long hands, the strong knuckles and the pink joints of his fingers. I wanted to reach out and take his hand in my own. I wanted to break his loneliness.

I breathed in to make myself brave enough to reach for him, and the faint sound of in-taken air made him look up at me.

I wished I hadn't seen the pain in his tense brow and bitten lower lip. I folded my arms and tucked my hands in my armpits.

Our little moment of something like friendship was gone. I might have asked him to name things for me in his language, so I could learn more of his words. We might have turned back and not seen a thing.

Instead, we stood there in silence.

And that was when we heard the first rush of fleet-footed animals on the move at the edge of the pasture farthest from us.

Unicorns are silent creatures, and I had never seen so many at once. An entire herd. There were fifteen at least. Far fewer than Torun's sheep, but somehow the group seemed fuller. These creatures had a subtle golden dapple to them, like the colour of sunlight through fall leaves or old parchment held up to a candle. Their horns were dark at the base and curved slightly up, like the blade of a sabre. The sound of them on the move was like the sound of a hand smoothing velvet, like pouring water over pebbles.

I wasn't near enough to see Sida among them, so I started to run towards them. Torun caught me around the waist with his long-fingered hands and drew me back behind a tree.

"Wait!"

His arms were narrow and muscular, but having touched me, he tried to keep space between us. I ducked under his arms and sprinted forward.

When I was three steps in, I stopped abruptly and was glad that Torun was frozen in his place behind me.

Sida was not among them. None of these *uksarv* were her particular quicksilver grey; none of them had her knobby knees or woolly coat. I shivered. These were all strangers to me.

And they were not pleased to see me. Halting their progress toward me with much stamping, the group of *uksarv* wheeled away. One peeled off the body and cantered towards me, head waving back and forth to see me better. The *uksarv* slowed and lowered its horn as the distance between us closed.

Heart thudding, I dropped down to my knees in the grass and held my arms out to show that I had no weapon, that I was vulnerable.

The *uksarv*, a doe, heaved out her breath. Spring pollen clouded the air between us.

I dared not make a sound. She was slight, thirteen hands at the shoulders, the size of a pony. Her flanks were scarred, a testament to many seasons of mating and motherhood. She circled me, and as she passed my back, I looked forward and noticed that the *uksarv* were all female.

She came around in front of me and stopped.

I reached my hand out, palm open, so she could see it was empty, so she could smell me. Perhaps Sida's scent clung to me under the stink of wool and wood smoke and human sweat. For a heartbeat, we were both still, watching each other breathe.

Suddenly, the herd sprang into motion. A lone, narrow, bristling-maned, barrel-chested buck was tearing towards them through the trees from the east. The buck gave a scream of masculine pride that was like the rip of an old branch tearing down the side of a tree.

My doe, the matriarch as I understood her to be, gave me one swift look with an amber eye and turned to meet the buck at full speed. She blocked him, and he veered sharply to the south. He tried to dodge her, but she diverted him with a prod from her horn on his left flank before he could throw back his hind heels. The matriarch gave a small rear and brought her fore-hooves down sharply and pawed the ground. The interloper backed away a few paces and then turned, striking back with his hind legs. The matriarch lowered her horn and chased him back, the buck attempting to kick back at her as he ran.

The matriarch took the opportunity of his flight to lead her does off to the east.

Forgotten, I edged backwards on my belly towards the woods. In breeding season, bucks were not to be provoked and this one was still too close for safety. Torun, pale and wide-eyed, grabbed me by the ankles and dragged me into the shade of the forest.

Crouching down, he flipped me onto my back.

"Are you hurt?" He leaned over me to pat my face, my arms.

"I'm fine," I said, sitting up.

He took my hands and pulled me up. I started to shiver.

Behind us, the buck screamed again. I looked over my shoulder. He had seen us and was rushing down the hill. Thwarted of his desire, the buck seemed intent on unleashing his fury on us.

I gave Torun's hands a tug and then dropped them. "Come on...Run!"

We couldn't run down such an incline, not really. We stumbled downhill, stepping swiftly over logs and between roots. I lost sight of the path.

The buck pursued us in a rage. Then—because we were not dead—I realized that something had changed. His pace had eased slightly. He had not run us down or stabbed us through with his horn, although he could have done so.

"He's tracking us," I gasped at Torun.

He nodded as we jogged on, our heels sliding in the dried needles and leaves on the forest floor. We were going too far towards the right, westward, so we tried to head east.

Through the trees, I saw that the buck had quickened his pace. His dun-gold body flashed against the dark trunks of the trees as he drew level with us on our left. He came near us until we hastily changed routes and veered right. Each time we tried to move east, he was there.

"He wants us to go west," Torun said. "He's *herding* us!"

My lungs were on fire, and now I felt my stomach contract. Why? Sida had run circles around me as a game and the matriarch had gathered her does, but what was this buck driving us to?

Ahead of us, the trees were thinning and we could see the sharp blue of the cloudless spring sky. Over the sound of our footsteps and our ragged breaths, I heard a rumbling rush.

Torun's pace slowed and he pulled me to a fast walk. The buck had led us to a steep cliff edge that overhung the river.

Behind us, the buck gave a whuffling sound, reminding us to move. I glanced over my shoulder. He was pacing back and forth, blocking any attempt at escape with his head lowered and his horn pointed.

The river was no longer the muddy, swollen storm of the first days of the melt. It ran clear, but the current still flowed fast. I looked at the edge of the overhang. Below us, there was a ten-foot drop to the river. No rocks that I could see. Not a fatal jump, I thought. The breeze lifted and I caught a whiff of something rotten and sulfurous, like bad eggs. The stink was at odds with the fresh smell of the river and the forest, but I had no time to think about its source.

The buck unicorn was considering us, swinging his head back and forth to gaze with one tawny eye and then the other.

"Can you swim?" Torun asked, looking at my boots. I hastily shrugged off my pack and pulled my boots off. If they filled with river water, no amount of strong swimming was going to bring me to the surface. And unlike Torun, I had not grown up next to a swiftly running river. Torun was barefoot, and his narrow, calloused feet were etched with sap and earth.

"We're going to have to jump far," he said.

But the buck's head had come up and his horn was pointed to the sky.

"We may not have to," I said. My heart beating fast as my thoughts aligned.

The buck seemed curious now, rather than angry. His pacing had stilled.

We had reeked with fear during our run, but faced between him and the river, we regained our wits. This likely seemed interesting to him.

I opened my arms and curled my open hands upwards.

"Hello," I said.

The buck took a few prancing, boastful steps towards me. There was now only a foot between us, and only half a step between us and the edge of the cliff. He was pompous and wanted to brag. He gave a little rear and struck the ground with his hooves.

Panicking, Torun grabbed my hand and pulled me back. I tripped into him, and as we tried to regain our footing, we stepped off the cliff.

Suddenly, we were falling, falling, looking up at the sky and then SMACK!

We hit the cold river water on our backs, knocking the wind from our lungs. In the force of the fall, I lost Torun's hand.

Stunned, I let the current take me for a few moments and it pushed me to the surface. I took a first screeching, painful breath. I kicked my legs, but it was hard to keep my head up. I opened my eyes to see Torun nearby. The current was taking us fast down the river and the eastern bank ahead curved in. He spotted me and swam a few strokes towards me.

"Can you kick?" he asked, hooking me under one armpit.

I nodded, and we struggled over to the right side of the river, where the current slackened and our feet hit a muddy, rocky river bottom. Torun let go of me and stood up. I crawled out on my hands and knees and collapsed on the dry grass. We were shivering, but the sun was warm on our wet skin.

"I am sorry," Torun said. "I should have stayed still."

"No," I rasped. "I should have explained what I was doing."

I looked north, but I could no longer see the place where we had jumped. Torun pulled me up and we started walking slowly along the riverbank. I started to shiver. Torun shucked off his vest and handed it to me. Though the shearling lining was damp, it had repelled much of the water. The outside was soaked, but the leather blocked the light wind.

We walked side by side, our hands swinging a little with each stride. My knuckles brushed the palm of his hand and he curled the tips of his fingers over mine. It was the most natural and intimate of actions.

I kept my breath quiet, not wanting to disturb whatever had formed between us.

He also did not seem willing to speak, so I thought more about what we had seen. Or what we had *not* seen. We had *not* seen Sida.

"The carving...did you make it after seeing *those*?" I said.

He shook his head. "I saw only one. She was small...between an *uksarv voon* and an *utta*."

"Then you saw Sida," I said.

Torun put into words what I was thinking. "Then where is she?"

I looked around. "And where are we?"

CHAPTER ELEVEN

Old Tales

We had washed up on the other side of the river, the Fenlen side. As we walked, the sun sank low and as the earth cooled, a mist had risen. I did not think we had gone so far, or even that we had been out for so long. But now, somehow, it was late. We stood still, both thinking the same thing. Night would fall and there was no way of getting home.

"Melina is going to be mad," I said.

He looked at me sharply. "Go mad?"

"She'll be angry," I clarified.

"Ah." He nodded. "Yes. And worried."

We lapsed into silence again. There was nothing to be done.

His hold on my hand tightened a little. "We should find some shelter."

The river was to our left, so we went right, stumbling over rocks until we found the face of the escarpment.

"We should not be here," Torun said. I said nothing. He was right—being lost in a forest at night made it harder to find your way out in the daytime.

We turned and walked a little. Torun stopped suddenly in front of a boulder. He dropped my hand.

"This is the place," Torun said.

"What do you mean?

"This is where we met."

"How can you be sure?" It looked like any boulder shaggy with moss.

"This is the rock on which I sat. After Bettina, I ran. This is where I stopped. If I went farther..." He took me around the side of the boulder and rubbed some moss away to reveal shallow, worn away lines in the rock face. The curves of eyelids, hollowed out pupils, a natural slash forming the mouth. "This is where people say the Alvina set their borders, according to the old stories. Melina told me if I crossed over, I would be lost." He shivered beside me. "If I believed in stories and in bad luck, this would be a sign. But I don't believe. Come on."

From the side of the boulder that was nearest to the forest, we made an arc southward. He seemed to know where he was going, even in the mist. Beside the boulder were a series of smaller stones curving south, like an arm. The last was slightly larger, a lump with a long extension pointing south, like a finger. I had not noticed any of these signs the first night—they had been obstacles underfoot, nothing more.

I saw another arm made of raised stones, pointing towards the forest. I wanted to follow it but went after Torun with hesitating steps. We were going south, along the ridge. I breathed in deep and my nose filled with the tang of rot, the same as I smelled when we fell from the cliff face. About ten paces down the path, there was another boulder. A hole for a mouth. Two slanting, suspicious eyes, the outline of a nose.

To our right lay another boulder, another face. The mist hid much from my eyes, but the path underfoot became wider, rockier, until it disappeared into a pile of rubble. We turned.

And there, shoulder high, was a break in the cliff face, revealing the snarling dark maw of the earth. Above my head were two holes carved out for eyes, two smaller ones for nostrils. The rocks were yellowed, and as I came closer to the cave, the colour deepened to an orange-red, like a huge, outspread mouth. The air reeked of sulphur. But the soles of my chilled feet warmed in the dirt. I curled my toes into the grit. It was as if the heat were coming from the ground.

"We shouldn't go close," Torun said.

"What is this place?"

"*Alvina birlan*. People go here to disappear." He opened his mouth as if to say more, but then fell silent.

Did this have something to do with *her*? I could not ask directly.

"It isn't safe, but we'll be warm from the breath of the cave." Torun sat down and crossed his arms over his raised knees. I settled a few safe feet away. It was too dark to pick wood for a fire and we had no flint or tinder anyway. But the rocks were heated by the bowels of the earth, and the soil was a rich and crumbling red streaked with veins of black.

"What is Alvina?" I asked.

"Not what. Who. It depends on who you ask. Some people say they are the old people who live in caves under the forest."

"Oh," I said. "Like the Old Folk?"

"What 'Old Folk?'"

"Well…" I began. Heat began to gather in my chest. "Never mind."

"No. Tell. What do *you* mean 'Old Folk?'"

"A kind woman told me stories about them when my father disappeared." I picked up crumbs of ruddy earth and ground them between my fingers. "She said they lived in the forest and lured away lonely travellers."

The corners of his mouth gave a skeptical twitch. "I did not think you are the person who believes those stories." The smile faded, and he dipped his chin to his chest. "You thought I was Alvina?"

"Well, I don't know!" I felt queasy with embarrassment. I had never thought to ask Torun more about the place into which I had come. "Well, then, what *are* you?"

"Verian. Like you are Gersan," he said simply, like he was sorting out chickens from geese. "That is our people's name. Our language. But there are not many of us. If you go further east, people start talking Philistre. That's what the queen and her ministers speak."

Of course, Torun and Melina were not magical...they were just *different*. But I felt stupid for not knowing anything about this place and these people. There was no hiding my ignorance now.

At the sight of my mortified face, Torun broke out laughing and then stopped abruptly. "Thinking as you did, you let me... lure...you? You thought I might be a dangerous creature and you came anyway?"

"Just at the beginning! I was lost and then suddenly you were there. Then the house in the tree...and it was all mixed up with"—I did not say Bettina's name—"and then I find Pa. After being just...gone...for so long." I hated saying such things aloud. The hurt felt like it should belong to another version of me.

The silence stretched out.

"So, if you thought I was Alvina, Melina would be the Alvina woman who has kept your father from you. If we were magical creatures, your heart would not hurt so much?"

Worse and worse. "It made a sort of sense at first. For why he never came back for my mother." My pulse was beating hard in my neck. I had never wanted to admit these things, even to myself. "My mother is beautiful, I think." It sounded so foolish; most girls thought their mothers were beautiful, if only in the vain knowledge that they would one day resemble them. Ma was forceful, that was closer to the truth, and I resented and admired her for it in a way Pa evidently did not. "No...Ma is strong. Somehow, he had just walked away from her." And from me.

"Hmmm." Torun looked at me askance. He had insisted yesterday that he was not trapped here, that he chose to stay. But I felt trapped, and not only by Sida's absence. I did not like having him look at me and know these things.

"Anyway, then I thought you could help me find Sida and not much else mattered after that." I looked up and around at the gaping cave mouth, where the shadows gathered. "Well," I said. "You are not Old Folk. I know that. And I am not Alvina. You know that." There was an uncertain pause and I pushed through it. "What are the Alvina, then? Who?"

"There are different types of stories," Torun said slowly. "Some people say that there was once a city here, hundreds of years ago. When our folk arrived, there was a battle, and the Alvina, the people who lived here, took refuge in a cave and never came out. And these stone faces are all that is left."

I looked up at the mouth of the cave. "And is this the place where they went underground?" I was beginning to understand why he didn't want to go any further.

"Maybe."

This story made sense to me. One of Victor's books, *The History of the Kings of Gersa*, described great carvings of chalk made in the hillsides of West Gersa, depicting bears and wolves. The book said they were left by giants; Ma said the carvings were left behind by earlier tribes whose names we had forgotten.

"In that story, either the Alvina found another world below the forest, or they are the ghosts of the dead and take revenge on our folk. We live in the trees, some old people say, to trick the Alvina. If they cannot find us, they cannot bring us bad luck. But they can be appeased with gifts of milk and bread and honey cakes."

I shivered. The lamb-girl...who looked like...who might be Bettina...had offered me just those things. But Torun wasn't done.

"Other people say that the Alvina were cruel to the forest and cut down sacred trees. Then Earth Mother became angry and swallowed the city. The cave is her mouth. The forest took back what was hers. They say the *uksarv* guard the forest and the Alvina, in punishment, must guide souls between the lands of the living and the dead. For us, everything on this side of the river belongs to the dead."

I shivered. "Is that why you don't graze your sheep there?"

Torun shrugged. "That's why we're the only house this far out. The grazing is good, but the other shepherds like to give the forest space. This place is so wild, they say, that the *uksarv* cross the river into our lands."

"But that doesn't explain..." I fell silent. How could *I* explain what had happened to me? "But there *is* something strange about..."

"About what? A cave that stinks of death?" Torun seemed oddly agitated. "Maybe this is just a place where people run away from life. Do you see a great king's city?"

I saw great boulders everywhere. There wasn't a city, but there wasn't anything that prevented me from imagining one here, either. I thought of the slash of autumn I had seen, the scream. What about the strange girl I had met in the forest so many years before? I thought about the impossible fact that Bettina and I were the same age, that Pa had walked back in time when he crossed the forest.

But Torun pressed on. "It doesn't mean anything."

"You know the tales well for someone who doesn't believe in them."

"You don't have to believe in a joke to find it funny."

Don't you? I thought. Don't you have to *want* to believe, just a little? But to say so would have made him clamp down on what he thought and said. Instead I asked, "How do you know the stories?"

"When I was little, after my parents died, I lived with Melina's parents. Her father told me stories when he taught me to herd. That was before your father came."

"Do you wish you were back there?"

He shook his head. "The old man's dead. He was good to me. The old woman...well, you'll meet her sometime." He didn't seem particularly happy about the idea. "The stories were good for me then. I needed them because I thought the Alvina made life better. Put out a honey cake for them and you have a good lambing season. But there's no such thing," he said bluntly. "There is just the world that we live in. Magic might belong to the trees and to the animals, but it does not belong to humans. Otherwise," he snapped a twig in half and threw it away from him. "Otherwise, things would be different." He visibly retreated into himself, shoulders pushing inward and up, chin tucking down.

It was a long, silent night.

CHAPTER TWELVE
Visiting

Melina was not impressed when we arrived home soaked through and shivering the next morning. We had waded across the river to get back. The water went up to our necks in places and fighting the current left us exhausted.

I was in great disgrace, and not only for having lost my pack and my boots. I could see from the uneasy expression on Melina's face that our accident confirmed the fears she had expressed in her argument with Torun the day before.

She sent me behind the curtain with Sarai and Telka so that I could change into a clean shift near the bed. Torun undressed in a nook that held sacks of barley and millet while Melina paced the main room. Under the mutter of Melina's voice, I could hear the pull of wet fabric over Torun's skin.

"*What happened?*" Sarai asked me. I didn't even have to think of translating the phrase in my head. I was starting to understand that much of...Verian. Verian, I reminded myself, was the name of their tongue. She hung my wet shirt and trousers over the line. "*So?*"

I was tired, cold and couldn't think of the right words.

"*Uksarv,*" I said.

"*Pfft*" was Sarai's typical reaction as she tossed me dry clothes.

"*UKSARV!*" Telka's eyes grew large. She snatched the little carved animal from under her pillow and began to trot it along the bed as I dressed. "*Uksarv, uksarv, uksarv...*"

There was a silence on the other half of the curtain.

"*Heirre.*" Come here, Melina was commanding us.

Torun was hunched over his porridge. Today it was savory, with flecks of meat in it. He caught my eye as I sat down across from him and then looked away.

I decided I would keep my face to my bowl. I ate a spoonful of creamy, salty porridge. Food had never tasted so good. I was being fed, though I had made Torun disappear for a day and night. I looked at Melina, who was moving around the house, reaching behind the loom, under the bed. I wanted to apologize but wasn't sure how. Or what I should apologize for. Going to the *Alvina birlan* had been an accident, after all. Perhaps the cave— and Melina's anger—were connected to Bettina? But that had been a year ago, and according to Torun, the Alvina were just a story. As I chewed, I failed to come up with the proper words.

Melina walked by the table with her arms full of rolled skirts, belts, pillowcases, plain bolts of cloth. She nudged Torun with her elbow, said "Torun, *kesilik*," and walked on without acknowledging me.

"Melina wants me to tell you that we need to go to the village to sell the cloths," he explained in Gersan. "They cannot wait for your father." Torun finally met my eyes. "I started to tell them about finding the *Alvina birlan*." He looked sidelong at Melina, who was giving instructions to Sarai. Rather mysteriously, he added, "And now we go sell."

"But what about finding Sida?"

He shook his head. "I will take you girls to the village first. This is family business. Without this, we go nowhere out of Melina's sight."

We?

"But the sheep?"

"Maro and Dan can be with them another day."

And so we spent a hurried hour laying out what we—by which I mean Melina, Sarai and Telka—had made. Dan came up to watch as they sorted the finer, more intricate productions where the plants had curling tendrils and the animals had sinuous necks, from those with geometric designs and raised puffs and cross loops made of thicker, rougher threads. To my surprise, it was the fine cloths that Torun packed into three bundles.

"Wouldn't it be better to sell the nicest ones to the people farther away?"

"No," Torun answered, heaving the largest bundle onto his back. "The village people deserve our best. We need their good will. The others…that is your father's business."

Was it defiance against Pa's willingness to put a price on things, or business sense? Perhaps piled, raised designs were harder to weave than I thought.

"We save patterns with meaning for those who can read them," Torun said as he stood. "Come."

We set out with Torun a few paces ahead with his bow and arrows, then Melina and Sarai with their cloths in handcarts, and then lastly me, with Telka clinging to my shoulders. After two hours, I was so tired that I did not realize when we had reached the village. We had passed through an odd sort of orchard with blossoming fruit trees mixed with different nut trees, a forest of edible things. Then the hard-beaten track had widened into a road and then a clearing, which suggested that we had come to a sort of meeting place. Somewhere, I heard the cluck of chickens. A voice called, high up above us, and Melina raised her face to answer.

I looked up and saw the carved and painted undersides of a portico spreading across the thick branches of the oak tree we had been passing under. While our portico was grey, weathered, unseasoned wood, these were patterned in interweaving lines of moss green, new leaf green, the green of a cat's eyes. From the painted motley flashed flowers and birds of red, yellow, purple. I had assumed that our—Melina's—house was in the trees because of the river. Now I thought of what Torun had told me.

"It's like in the story," I said, looking up. "People living in the branches."

A door opened upwards from the portico floor and a set of wooden stairs was lowered down to us. Melina went up, followed by the girls. I hung back. I had been half hoping for a bustling, anonymous marketplace. I had not expected to enter our customers' homes, nor to measure how our life compared to those around us.

"Torun!" Melina called.

He gestured towards the stairs. "You first."

"Why not you?"

He grinned. "I need to push you if you are too afraid."

"I am not," I said, and I stumbled up the stairs.

I stopped at the top, knee poised at the portico floor. A family had gathered around Melina and the children and was staring at me. Smiles faded, cheeks paled. A girl my age lifted her hand to her mouth before self-consciously letting it drop and attempting to smile at me. An ancient woman with the face of a prune and a collapsed, toothless mouth was less subtle in her manner. She brought her left forefinger and thumb to her forehead and heart, a sign to ward off evil.

"That is Melina's mother," I hear Torun whisper. "She is our family's *Velni-Ani*. The Old-Mother." I felt Torun's fingers tentatively push the heel of my poised foot forward.

Blushing, I scrambled onto the portico and smoothed my skirt. Torun climbed up nimbly, and the stares shot from me to him. He came to the family and kissed them each on the right cheek and reminded Melina in the lightest of tones that they had a full day ahead of them. He opened his arms and ushered them back inside, unconsciously taking up the motions of a shepherd.

A question broke free from the mother, concerning me no doubt, and the heads began to turn my way. Torun kept walking them inside, but he looked at me and nodded me towards them.

Once they had gone in, Torun held out his hand to me. "Come. They are cousins. Rina is our age and kind. The first will be the worst. You will get used to the looks."

From my place by the stairs, I didn't believe him. But banter soothed me, so I asked, "How do you know?"

"I have had practice." He bent his fingers to urge me to come.

I began walking towards him and reached out my hand. "What practice?" As soon as the words left my mouth, I wished I could have bit off my tongue. Of course, after Bettina's...whatever it was...death or disappearance...Torun's sorrow would have been keenly watched over and gossiped about.

Torun's hand dropped, and he stepped away from me. His pale eyebrows rose above his dark eyes. His mouth hardened. "Just ask Melina how you can help. If you can't, just mind Telka."

But Telka scampered off to play with the other children while Melina spoke in hushed tones with the older women. They bustled about through the house, collecting things. Sarai held me gently by the billowed sleeve of my shirt.

Torun sat in a corner with his shoulders up, clearly disapproving. He once tried to speak up to one of the women, but they cut him off and sent him outside. I looked over my shoulder as he stalked out and saw a group of young men calling to him. One had the clay-smeared sleeves of a potter's apprentice, and another wore the leather apron of a blacksmith. The door swung shut.

What lay before me did not seem like any market venture I had ever seen.

Under the direction of her mother and grandmother, Rina

laid out a sheet and poured poppy seeds on it in a narrow line and gestured that I should step over them. I did, and she gathered the poppy seeds together.

The women held out objects made of iron—cooking pots, knives, a nail. I took each one in turn and handed it back.

They gave me a spoon and a shallow bowl with a pottage made of meat and barley.

The old woman—my half-siblings' grandmother, Velni-Ani—grabbed my wrist and turned my palm upwards. She ran her fingers over the creases, stained with sap and dust from my walk with Telka. She gave a "hmph," curled my fingers over my palm and returned my hand to me.

Velni-Ani called Melina and the two muttered amongst themselves. Rina signalled Sarai over and gave her a red cord with a small iron pendant on it, a simple hollow disk. Sarai ran back and tied it around my neck, snagging a few hairs in the knot. "This to sell cloth?" I asked in my childish Verian, rubbing my neck. I was going to have to get Torun to teach me how to speak better. After so many years of Ma insisting that I speak Gersan properly, it was painful to know how bad I sounded in Verian. I looked around to make sure no one else had heard. They hadn't. The women were happily picking through the rolls of cloth Melina had brought up.

Sarai shook her head. "This is for you, before we sell to others. This shows you don't have evil spirits living in you." Her lip curled.

My face felt hot as I thought about what Torun had said, about Alvina taking revenge and causing bad luck. But I was Pa's daughter, there was nothing supernatural about that!

"I...Pa..." I felt stupid. Why was speaking so much harder than understanding? From the expression on Sarai's face, I couldn't tell whether she scorned me or the old woman. I saw

Rina watching me, almost apologetically. She seemed too shy to come over. I wondered whether she and Bettina had been friends. It seemed likely.

"You came at twilight and you say you were lost. You fell in the river and Torun fell with you. You found the cave and slept there. You might be unlucky for us to keep. An *Alvinaisik*."

An Alvina girl? I needed to bring Sarai to reality. "I think… we come to sell?"

Sarai gave me an edgewise look, as if remembering her craft made her dislike me less. "That too. But now we have to show you around because talk spreads fast."

The family visit was not the worst part of the day. Melina's mother's and sister's family had learned to respect Torun's silence and Melina's pain; others had not.

When we climbed down, each household of the village had gathered in the clearing below and had set up a bench of goods. Torun and Telka manned our handcarts, while Melina and Sarai took me around from bench to bench.

At every successive family that we visited, there were more open exclamations of surprise. Across the little marketplace, Torun became stiffer and more taciturn. Soon, he barely looked at me, and the only way I knew he kept watch over me was because I never saw him looking in my direction. His determination not to chat, not to smile, not to eat what they offered us—in short, to do nothing but business—made our family, him, me, the centre of gossip.

Melina and Sarai gave shorter and shorter explanations, none of which I could hear because they whispered them to their clients as cloth changed hands in exchange for earthenware, pearls of barley, chestnut flour, honey, a leather satchel, a set of needles. Telka was, blessedly, too young to care and soon ran off to play. I realized that Melina had brought her along as a test of my likeness.

I was mute with embarrassment. I, who could challenge manor-born Julian in perfect Gersan, now had an infant's vocabulary. Despite all the writing lessons Ma had put me through, I could not say what I was, who I was.

All the women and men and children walking by or stopping at our wares had to do was look at Torun and then look at me before making the ward sign. I heard one old woman tell another that I must be an *Alvinaisik*. The other jerked her chin at my iron amulet. I could feel the suspicion seething in the minds of the housewives who stepped away quickly with tablecloths and wall hangings in their baskets.

In the mid-afternoon, the trade died down. As we packed up, I heard the muffled outbursts of opinion from the porticos as they watched me retreat. Torun kept packing our purchases more tightly, so they wouldn't rattle loose on the way home.

When we were ready to leave, we found Telka in the middle of a circle of children, telling them about the many *uksarv* who lived around her home and how Torun and I would bring one for her as a pet.

"*Chut!*" Sarai waded into the troop of children and scooped Telka up under the arms. Sarai dragged her towards our cart. Telka giggled and waved to her friends. One of the little boys pointed at me and Telka nodded vigorously.

As we left the clearing, someone called out "*Ufoli sheled!*" Sarai looked up to glare. Torun did not, but his shoulders were high and tight.

"Ignore them, Sarai. I'll take care of it later."

"Pfft. Don't, Torun. It'll make it worse."

"What did they say?" I broke in.

"They called you a foreign...brat," he said. I suspected that brat was a rather loose translation for *sheled*. We walked home in silence. Sarai forged ahead with the bow and arrow, while

Melina and Torun, pushing the handcarts, were deep in con-
templation of I know not what. Telka rode in Torun's cart, tired
and content to stare at the sky through the early spring leaves.

I walked in between Sarai and the handcarts, caught between
tears of relief and disappointment. Relief that it was over, disappointment in myself because, after all, why would I expect a
kinder reception from the village? What had I wanted? I was a
fool. My half-siblings had accepted me because of my father. But
the village was not beholden to my father and I was no part of
their blood. So why should I be anything but an outsider?

I noticed that Sarai had stopped ahead of me. I ran up to her.
Had she seen something?

Looking down, she hadn't spotted anything, except her
brown, smudgy toes. Her shoulders hunched and the tendons
in her neck were strained.

"Sarai?"

She burst into tears. I edged away, feeling that I was the
cause of her anger. All day, I had done nothing right. At least I
could give her space.

"No," she said, putting a hand on my arm and withdrawing
it as soon as I stopped my retreat. Sarai had never touched me
voluntarily and I was surprised to feel how light and narrow her
hand was. No wonder she was a nimble weaver.

"It's not fair," she said, slowly so that I could understand.
"You didn't do anything. It's not your fault you look like Bettina.
You aren't anything like her and you can't talk better than Telka,
but they shouldn't stare at you for that."

"Why I not her?" Although I could understand Verian, my
ability to speak it failed me at this crucial moment. I had asked
the question the wrong way. Or perhaps mangling the words
wasn't that bad of a thing because Sarai sniffed, rubbed her nose
with the back of her hand and shook her tear-damp hair out of

her face. "Because you're a terrible weaver," she said, her composure regained. Apparently, Sarai had exclusive rights to criticize me and guarded her rights jealously.

She cleared her throat. "They think you are a little *bivin*." I frowned, not understanding the last word. She made her eyes big and growled and made her hands into claws. "*Bivin*...Like an animal."

Wild, I thought. They think I'm wild.

My language made me a child or an idiot. A domesticated, obedient idiot might not be too bad, but I was a wild one. At least Sarai didn't seem to mind.

"I told them you are no use at the loom. I think you will be more useful by being where you are happy. In the woods."

Useful. That was the important word for Sarai, not happy.

I looked over my shoulder, where I saw Melina and Torun stopped a few paces behind us. "What you need?" I asked. I didn't have the words to be anything but blunt.

A strange ripple passed over Sarai's face, something like surprise or pleasure.

"I want colour," she said, pointing to the threads in her skirt. "Red. Blue. Green. Yellow. And...and more. Colours no one else has. And flowers," she said running her fingers over the shapes on her belt.

"I bring flowers," I said, in my best efforts at Verian. "I bring red. Blue. Green."

Sarai's pale face flushed slightly, as if in some private triumph, and she strode down the path ahead.

That night, I stood in the field by the river under the full moon.

"Sida," I whispered, hoping that she was nearby. "Sida!"

I saw nothing. Sida did not return; she had gone elsewhere and I would have to find her.

CHAPTER THIRTEEN

The Herd

I walked, watched, waited. Sida would reveal herself, but I could not know when.

I settled into a pattern of wandering through the forest trails in the day and coming home with some berries or plants I had found for Sarai. Woad and larkspur for blue, dyer's rocket for yellow, crottle lichen for orange. As darkness fell, I helped card wool, or chop wood, or cook.

I followed Torun's tracks, venturing a little farther here or there, until I found the ledge where the buck had scared Torun into pulling us into the river. My boots and pack were lying there, scattered over with dirt and dried pine needles, like the souvenirs of a suicide. My feet had grown tough with barefooted ramblings, so I tied my boots together with a bit of twine and slung them over my neck. They would be useful when the weather turned cool. I was very happy to find my pack, with its emergency supplies. If I ever had the chance to go home, the pack would help me leave.

I hadn't crossed the river since my fall with Torun and the night by the cave. I wondered whether this forest, too, belonged to Fenlen. It was wild and nobody except Torun and the sheep seemed to come here. I did not cross the river because I knew Sida was on the east bank.

One day, I was hiking up to the high pasture where Torun stayed overnight with the herd after the lambs had dropped. I tried to go there every other afternoon or so for a few hours, and he taught me words and phrases. I muttered yesterday's lesson to myself as I climbed over logs and picked my way through saplings that had recently grown thick with leaves.

"This mutton tastes good," I said to myself in Verian. "Please give me more mutton. How old is that sheep?" I was conscious of being shadowed through the forest, but I pretended I hadn't noticed a thing. I was almost at the pasture.

I named the things around me, refusing to turn at the sound of a mushroom being crushed. "Tree. Tree. Tree. Leaf. Bird. Pine tree. Rock. Big rock. Little rock. Many rocks."

I hoped it would be Sida, but I was curious about the other creatures I had seen. I stopped where I was.

There was a scurry of movement. In front of me, as if from nowhere—I swear I had been watching the path—the barrel-chested buck charged past me on the right.

"*Uksarv.*"

Ahead, I saw Sida leap into sight as she galloped by me on the left, far up the hill. The buck gained ground and suddenly Sida stopped, looked over her shoulder and kicked, nailing him in the cheek with a hoof. He stumbled to the side and...disappeared.

Instead of wondering how a large animal had vanished, seemingly into thin air, I lost my self-control and shouted after Sida.

"Sida! Sida, come back here!" I chased her, but she was much swifter, especially uphill.

I paused at the edge of the pasture.

Sida stood in front of Torun, who was kneeling in front of her with his hands outstretched and upturned. He had observed me closely that day on the cliffside, I realized. Sida smelled him, rested her cheek to his. Carefully, slowly, with his hands still out, Torun stood up. Sida rubbed her nose on his right hand and he gently stroked the side of her face.

Sida loved attention and had recently had none. She tilted her head up so he could get at the angle between her head and neck.

Torun stepped backwards and Sida stepped forward, so as not to lose any scratching. He sang to her softly as he went.

I felt a surge of jealousy. Why hadn't I thought of singing?

I jogged up towards them, panting and very confused. She had been avoiding me, so why...but my thoughts of myself faded as I came closer.

Besides the big gash I had noticed, Sida now bore a myriad of small cuts and lesions, as if she had been running through sharp boulders and raspberry thickets.

"*Chuuu*," Torun murmured, as he stroked her sides. "*Chuuu*."

"The buck was running after her."

He looked over to me. "It happens sometimes with the sheep, with rams and ewes," Torun said in Gersan. "Is the buck near?"

I shook my hand. "She kicked him and he...he went off." I couldn't understand quite where, though.

"Good. Fetch some water, please," he said, checking her hooves. "And my bag."

When I handed his bag and flask to him, I saw that Sida's gash was mostly healed, but there were a few places where the skin still stretched a reddish pink and where the scabs oozed and cracked. Torun kept stroking her with one hand, rooting through his bag with the other. He took out some dried herbs and put them into his mouth.

"*Yimma naisik*," Torun murmured. Good girl. To me, he said, "There should be some vinegar there."

As he chewed, Torun washed her cut, first with water and then with vinegar. To my amazement, Sida's ears flicked back and forth, but she didn't shy away from him. With one hand, he scooped the herbs out of his mouth and spread them into the cut.

"That could infect her!" I said.

"Do you have a better idea?" he said in his calm voice. "I do this with my sheep. And myself."

"I have some alicorn ointment," I said. I upended the bag and everything tumbled out, including balled-up lint, apple seeds and stems, a small jar of alicorn ointment my mother insisted I carry everywhere and a chipped-off old bit of horn.

Torun paused in his ministrations. "What…"

I tossed the horn back in and began packing with great speed and precision.

"Was that…?"

"Yes," I said as calmly as I could. "It's nothing. I sometimes find them in the forest."

"Don't let anyone see it," Torun said.

"I'm not stupid." Huffily, I grabbed the jar of ointment.

Sida would not let me come near her with it. I stepped forward, she stepped back. I stepped to the right, she stepped left. I set it down. "I suppose it would be odd to be healed with a part of your own body," I conceded.

"Do you have any rope?" Torun asked. "She might be safer if she stays here."

I found a length in my pack, but when Sida saw me tie a loop on the end of it, she reared up a little and then bucked.

"Sida, this is for your safety," I said.

She lowered her head, and if she had grown a horn of any size, she might have been dangerous.

I dropped the rope. "Or not. I'm not sure we would be any help against a buck."

"True. If we give her something she wants, perhaps she will stay. What does she eat?" Torun asked.

"At first it was milk from our goats. Then she used to eat oats and barley cooked in milk, she was just starting on new flowers and grass…" I trailed off. Sida wasn't a baby anymore. She had been feeding herself for some time now.

"Well, what do other *uksarv* eat?"

"They're picky. Wild plums, new leaves, bark off certain trees. But it's not predictable."

Torun stroked Sida's neck. "Then we should leave her to make her own choices."

"But she might run off and never come back!" My voice was tight with fear.

Torun turned towards me and put a hand very lightly on my shoulder, near my neck. "She came back to you," he said. "Trust her."

I found myself biting back strange fears.

Torun moved his hand to pat me on the back. Pat-pat. Pause. Pat-pat. He paused again and put his arm around my shoulders in an uncertain attempt at comfort.

"What if she doesn't need me anymore?" I mumbled. "What if she disappears?"

I felt Torun swallow. "Then she has chosen for herself. But I do not think she will do so."

We stood like that until my breathing stilled. When I opened my eyes, Sida was watching us curiously.

Sida leaned over and licked the tears from my face. She snuffled at the taste and I laughed at the slobber of it.

Then she took three steps backwards and trotted a circle around us. I reached out for her. "Come here, Sida…" She tore off through the meadow. The flock scattered and re-formed in small clusters.

"You are too afraid," Torun said. I would have run after her, but his arm dropped to my hand and he slowed my pace to a smooth walk.

We followed her and she went further down, running and then pausing at the edge of the forest. She watched us expectantly.

"She wants us to chase her," I said. "It's her old game."

"I'm going to have to bring the flock with me if we go farther,"

Torun said. We both thought about the mess of getting a herd of sheep through unknown terrain.

"You stay," I said. "She'll keep me safe."

"Come back after," he said. "Promise?"

"I promise," I said over my shoulder.

I followed Sida down through the forest.

She had grown wiser, leaving fewer tracks, but I could still see the scuff of overturned leaves here, a broken stick there. No Sida, just trees and trees and more trees. A rock. I sat down, breathed in. What had she wanted me to see?

I head a whicker to my right. I turned slowly, my heart beating hard.

It wasn't her.

I found myself facing a doe. Her dappling was darker than the others I had seen and a spray of gold-brown spots marked her cheeks and muzzle. The curve of her belly showed that she was heavily pregnant; a few more weeks and she would lose her horn before she gave birth. She seemed to belong to the group Torun and I had seen. In fact, though I dared not take my eyes off her, I thought I could see the rest of the does somewhere beyond me in the forest. Was Sida there? I could see, beyond the herd, a shifting patch of shadow. She was not quite amongst them, but they weren't chasing her away, either. I crouched slowly.

Here was the matriarch as well, slight and scarred. I noticed that one of her eyes had the slight milky sheen of a forming cataract. The freckled doe was her second-in-command in leading the herd.

The two circled me, their horns touching my face, my neck, drawing a line down my torso. They were testing me.

Then the matriarch stepped closer with her head up and I felt the velvety soft skin of her chin and lips and the prickle of her chin hairs as she considered my taste.

She turned her head to the side to feel the fast beat of my pulse. She stepped away.

I remembered my wad of Sida's hair in my pocket and carefully took it out.

"Please..." I held it out in my hand so they could look at it and smell it. Sida had been angry at me when I had grabbed this scrap of her, but it showed the matriarch that I had been close to her, not just today, but another time. Many times. I wanted to show them I was trustworthy.

The old matriarch seemed thoughtful. The younger, speckled doe stepped from side to side—as close to a prance as her belly allowed. Her ears pricked back and forth. I could not tell if she thought Sida was the threat, or me, who held the traces of a wounded unicorn. The matriarch shook her head and led the young doe off to the rest of the group. I did not try to follow them now and they pushed into the green of the forest. They stepped more carefully than Sida and left no tracks behind them. I felt alone and confused.

Would Sida be served better if I protected her from these *uksarv*, or was the idea of separating her from them somehow wrong? She had fled the buck, but these does clung together and protected one another.

If Sida joined these beasts who seemed to belong to this part of the forest, how could I get home? Perhaps I didn't need her at all. But then, if I got home and a hundred years had passed, Sida would be the only one I knew. Then what?

I walked back to Torun and the flock.

When I got there, up the field north of me, I saw Torun checking the tiny hooves of one of the lambs. He bent the animal's small legs in a perfunctory manner, lifting here, pressing there. But when he was done, he kissed the top of its head and made the ward sign between its ears. Unconscious of the favour, the lamb grunted and trotted away to its mother. Torun remained crouched where he was, squinting, thinking. In the afternoon sun, his shadow was long and cool in the grass. I sat down next to him with a thump and lay down in the grass with my knees up. I hugged myself.

"Any luck?"

I shook my head. The sky was so bright and blue that I had to close my eyes. I told him what I had seen.

"No sign of the buck?" he asked.

"Just the does…"

"That sounds like luck to me. She has found her herd. She will be safe with them."

But *I* was supposed to be her herd, I wanted to tell him. If she went, where did that leave me? Torun sat next to me in silence, letting me muddle through my thoughts. I heard him kick up a stick with his toes. A few seconds later, he took out his knife to carve.

I opened my eyes a slit. He sat blocking the sun. His back curved as he whittled.

"Are there any stories about *uksarv*?" At home, the story was that a young girl could lure a unicorn—pure of body and all that. I suspected the story wasn't exactly true, but it wasn't untrue either. Like the story of the Alvina, perhaps there was a kernel of knowledge, something to chew on.

"I'll warn you, it's not a very good one."

I closed my eyes again. "The story? I'll judge for myself."

"Yes," Torun said. He cleared his throat. "In the early days, Sun Father looked down on Earth Mother. She grew warm and in her belly a seed stirred. This was the Life Tree, which grew strong under the gaze of Sun Father. Sun Father and Earth Mother created many children between them. They grew on the branches of the Life Tree if they were animals and pushed upwards from the roots if they were plants. From the Tree grew a branch that drooped to the ground and from the branch grew a great flower and when the flower blossomed, in it was a Milk-White Mare."

"When are we getting to the *uksarv*?"

"Be patient! You're as bad as Telka. So. Earth Mother's dearest child was her Milk-White Mare. But Lightning watched the Milk-White and wanted her for its own. Though Lightning can touch what is on Earth, it cannot stay long. The Milk-White Mare was struck by a tongue of Lightning. Burned and hurting, she hid under the Life Tree, where the roots grew around her. Milk-White was the first creature to return to her mother, and now all creatures who tire of life come back to her."

"That's a story about death, not *uksarv*."

"*Chut*. I am not done. After many months, a new creature emerged alone from the hollow under the Life Tree. The Mare's Son was strange, like his mother in most ways, but bearing fire on his forehead. He chased the animals and women and men away from the Life Tree. The people forgot about the Life Tree and wandered away to other lands. Now the Life Tree creates in silence and secrecy and we cannot know it."

He was quiet again and all I could hear was the maaah-maaaah of the sheep and the breeze rustling through the tall grass. I sat up. "That's all?"

He shrugged.

"But that story's not anything like the *uksarv* we saw."

"Stories don't have anything to do with anything real. They're ways of saying things you can't say."

"What do you mean?" The part about the mare hiding under the Life Tree...it seemed to fit somehow with the story he told me about the Alvina and the cave. "What can't you say?"

He must have found my question unnerving because he

grunted, flicking a slice of white wood away from himself. "They're mostly nonsense." As he shifted, I got a good look at Torun's belt. It had a repeating pattern of paired black birds facing each other against an undyed, grey-white background. But in the dull cream of the wool, my eyes sometimes caught a glint of a brighter hair.

"Torun, when you think a story is a good one, I'll weave you a belt with peacocks dancing across it."

I closed my eyes, but the heat on my face told me he had shifted to look at me better. The sunlight made me see the lace-work of veins on my eyelids.

"Do you know what that means?" he said.

"It's a joke," I said. "If I weave you a belt, it will be all one colour. Probably brown."

"Hmm." He whittled in silence after that.

CHAPTER FOURTEEN

Rina's Wedding

I hadn't been paying attention when we went to sell cloth at the village. Or else I hadn't been able to read the signs. I couldn't understand that the stitching of red ribbon from the shoulder to cuff of new shirts for Sarai and for me meant something more than new shirts. I didn't catch on to the significance of baking nut rolls in the small clay-and-brick oven in the summer kitchen. Sarai slapping my hand away from them didn't mean a thing beyond her usual bad temper. But two days after the stories of the Milk-White Mare and her son, Torun came down with the herd in the midmorning.

"I'm down for the wedding," he said by way of explanation.

"What? Who?"

"Rina, of course. Didn't you know?" he asked with a wry smile as he sat down to a late breakfast. "It's all the girls could talk about before I left."

Torun added that Maro and Dan would take care of the flock in the little pasture underneath the house. They were not of marriageable age and so they did not have to come. Uninterested in dancing or ceremony, the boys accepted the task of watching the sheep for two days with glee.

"I can stay. I don't dance," I said. "I like sheep."

"Maybe you've never danced with the right person," Torun said lightly. And then he gave something that tried to be a wink but was more an exaggerated blink. I snorted.

"Torun, *heirre*." Melina called him away. "Lizbet…" with a jerk of her chin, she gestured towards the door. There was no way I was being left unsupervised.

When we reached the village, Torun drifted away to the bachelor house where the unmarried men were mourning the departure of Rina's groom. We had come a day early to help Rina in her preparations. But Rina was not arrayed as I thought a bride-to-be should be. When we came into the house, Rina sat in a corner facing the wall, wearing a ragged old shift. She did not turn around when we entered and neither Sarai nor Melina nor Telka looked her way. I tried to greet her, but Sarai tugged me away.

"No," she said. "Not yet."

I felt a prickle of uncertainty but was distracted by Velni-Ani's wrinkled scowling.

"Your *ufoli* husband is here, Melina," she said to her daughter, sending us out as soon as we had set down our bundles. "Make sure you're back for sunset."

Pa was at the clearing, where the tables for the wedding were being erected. He was proudly hawking the last of his wares, items that were less intricate than the ones Melina had brought before. To my surprise, people looked over the cloth and even bought a few pieces. When he saw us, however, he let the buyer take his last tablecloth without haggling.

He knelt down and spread his arms for Telka to run into. "*Telka-Voon!*" He peppered the top of her head with kisses and lifted her up. His love for her seemed genuine, perhaps because she was too young to be saddled with expectations. Sarai's mouth was a firm line; she wanted to know how the business went.

"Your cloths sold well. Heino has taken orders in advance. He's around here somewhere. But Sarai, I couldn't do it without you. So, guess who will be the handsomest girl?" He put a hand in the pouch that hung from his belt and pulled out a necklace of red, translucent beads. Sarai's characteristic stiffness unbent into a smile as she fastened the glossy strand around her neck. Grudgingly, I wondered if they might be of amber, or even garnet.

Melina walked toward him with slow dignity and Pa set Telka down to embrace his wife and kiss her. She whispered in his ear and he nodded. His eyes flicked towards me.

I crossed my arms, unwilling to be bribed.

"Elizabeth." He smiled and offered me nothing.

"Pa. Did you get to send word to Ma?"

His eyebrows lifted and his mouth sagged open slightly.

"You forgot."

"I didn't know how, ducky. No one I talked to has even heard of Gersa." He kissed the side of Melina's face again. I felt a sting in my nose, but I did not cry. If I was to return to Ma, it would be entirely through my own pains.

With a sigh, I consigned myself to a day of being overtly ignored and secretly examined. Torun was nowhere I could go, so I found Telka and played at being frogs on the portico, shouting "*Gorongos! Gorongos—HUP!*" and leaping until Velni-Ani stumped out to kiss her granddaughter and glare at me.

"I've lived too long," she said, "if I've lived to see an *Alvinaisik* passing as human."

Telka looked at me askance at hearing me called an *Alvinaisik*, an Alvina girl.

"I'm not an *Alvinaisik*," I retorted. "I'm an *ufoli sheled!*"

Velni-Ani gave a dry bark of laughter and pointed at Telka with her cane. "Put her to bed, *Alvinaisik*. If you want to be human, learn that you can't sass your elders."

"Are you an *Alvinaisik?*" Telka asked.

"No. Just your sister."

Velni-Ani shook her head. "Come on. We're about to get started."

As the sun began to set, the women and marriageable girls of the village gathered at the base of Rina's house. As they waited for Rina to emerge, they sang a song—first together and then in overlapping groups—until I, too, knew the words:

I'll walk away, away on the long road,
Make myself a coat from the dust of the long road.
From my sorrow and my shame, I will spin the thread,
Sew on buttons made of all, all the tears I've shed.
Blow away the dust, good wind, blow away the dust,
With my heart's old sorrow, take it to the dusk.

I felt I knew the tune from somewhere, and with a jolt, I recognized the tune as the song the lamb-girl had sung when I was very small. The melody was lovely, but I thought the words were far too sad, too eerie for a wedding. But no one else seemed to think so. In fact, the song seemed to fit their strange behaviour.

Rina stood up from her corner and Melina threw a blanket over her. I wondered aloud how she was going to make it down the steps all smothered up, but no one seemed willing to answer my questions. As the crowd moved along down the road, I noticed that Sarai had an additional shift flung around her neck like a scarf and that other women brought spare articles of clothing. A white-shawled widow pushed a wheelbarrow that carried something bulky that was, like Rina, smothered in blankets.

We walked out past the orchard beside a stream. The women and girls formed circle and Rina stood at the centre. From outside the circle, the widow and another older woman unwrapped the shape in the wheelbarrow.

It was a tall bundle of branches and sticks with twiggy arms protruding from the sides. On the top, someone had pulled a sack and painted a red, budlike mouth and two sooty eyes. Long strands of hay had been stitched to the top in rows. The weight of the hair pulled the face back and the stick-spine poked at the effigy's baggy throat.

I looked at Sarai for explanation. "It's a *hekunaisik*," she said. *Heku* meant wood, I knew. A wooden girl. "The old women made it for Rina. It's the other bride."

"What?"

"*Chut!*"

Rina stood in front of the wooden girl and combed her fingers through her long, wheat-gold hair to catch a few loose strands. She twisted the long threads together. These she wove into the stiff hair of the effigy. Rina cupped her hands in front of her mouth and breathed. Keeping her hands together, she placed them on the rough face and spread out her fingers, as if pressing her spirit into the doll. Last, Rina pulled the shift from her body and, standing naked in the circle of girls and women, pulled it over the stick's form.

The two old women still held onto the *hekunaisik*.

Sarai stepped forward and gave Rina her own spare shift, though it was short and tight in the shoulders. Another girl gave Rina a skirt. Another provided a belt. The widow holding the *hekunaisik* untied the white kerchief she wore and tied it around Rina's hair. Rina stepped back to stand between Melina and her mother.

"Now Rina is not herself, but all of us," Sarai whispered.

The old women turned the *hekunaisik* from side to side, as if it were alive and looking around. They lifted it and brought it forward, in front of Velni-Ani. One of the women twitched the rough head to one side, as if it were asking a question.

Velni-Ani said something, using words I did not know. The circle laughed and Rina blushed at her grandmother's words.

The puppeteers made the *hekunaisik* nod jauntily, and they stumped it to the next married woman. The women egged each other on, shouting out advice. The vocabulary was beyond me, but even Sarai gave a snort of laughter.

I shivered. Each jerky movement of the stick-bride was a parody of Rina's mannerisms—her shy, small movements made coquettish and knowing. At the end of the circle, the other women gathered close around Rina and the *hekunaisik* so that they were indistinguishable in the crowd. When we got back to the house, Rina's grandmother laid the *hekunaisik* in Rina's bed, and Rina slept between me and Sarai on the floor.

The next morning, the *hekunaisik* stood propped up in the main room as Rina dressed. Rina's long, thick hair was braided with ribbons and Telka braided ribbons into the rough hair of the *hekunaisik*. Rina wore a simple white shift, a good one today. The women wrapped a skirt around her, one that I recognized as one of Sarai's designs. Roses and budding thorns alternated against a pink background, bringing out the matching flush in Rina's cheeks. When I asked Sarai, she shook her head. "Bettina's," she said. On the very edge of the skirt, I recognized the faint glimmering thread of a unicorn hair, my good-luck gift to a strange girl from long ago. Not an elf-girl at all, but Bettina.

I felt slightly sick. So, I *had* met her.

I opened my mouth to say something, anything, but Sarai handed me a second skirt of the same pattern for the *hekunaisik*. Rina tied on two woven belts, one wrapped tight to show her waist, the other loosely knotted around her hips. Telka fastened the effigy's skirt with a bit of rope.

When the time came for the ceremony, Velni-Ani gave me the job of holding the *hekunaisik* as the community gathered in the clearing. I felt a little rush of hope—perhaps this role was a token of her acceptance? But my hope faded quickly. The *hekunaisik*'s spreading arms made it clumsy and I was at the edge of the bridal group.

Torun was standing with the other young men and, like them, was wearing a felted jacket instead of his usual vest. It was a fine garment worn for the occasion, but not the weather. When he saw me, he walked straight over. My eyes caught on his simple belt of matching birds. The gleaming thread...Bettina's handiwork, I thought. But I did not want to mention Bettina right before the ceremony.

Torun's face was pink from the heat.

"How long do I have to hold this?" I tried to make my tone one of jest, but I did not like being singled out with a weird, witchy object like the *hekunaisik*.

Torun looked furious. "Who let you touch that thing?" The vehemence of his words surprised me.

"Velni-Ani. I'm supposed to hold it for...well, I'm not actually sure."

He gave an angry grunt. "I can't believe Melina would let her."

He took it from my hands and leaned it against a tree. "It's an insult to have you associated with it. Usually they just prop it up by the feast table."

"Why? Torun, what is a *hekunaisik* for?"

"It's a stupid superstition. At a wedding, if the Alvina try to steal Rina away, they will steal the *hekunaisik* instead."

A sick feeling gathered in my stomach. I looked at the effigy lolling against the tree trunk. It seemed to look back at me. "Sarai said the old women made it for her."

Rina's betrothed, Giron, was gesturing at Torun to come over. "Just...stay away from it. Please?" Torun sighed and stepped away.

Somewhere, in front of us, someone began to beat a small

drum. I wriggled my way through to Sarai and Telka. Stepping out from a cluster of maidens, Rina threw off her enveloping blanket. She and her groom approached each other. I heard the hum of a stringed instrument. I looked behind me for the source of music. The drummer, a scrawny boy Maro's age, sat with his instrument between his legs, a slender rod in one hand, a stick topped a fist-sized ball in the other. Sitting beside him, an old woman was holding what looked vaguely like a fiddle carved out of a single piece of wood. On the drummer's other side stood an equally old man with a long reed pipe. The piper made a ward sign when he saw me watching him, so I looked back to the couple.

Sarai was just stepping back with a cup of sheep's milk. A bit of white clung to the faint hairs above Rina's upper lip—I had evidently missed some blessing. The piper, who seemed to have overcome his brush with the *ufoli sheled*, began to play a shrill, lively tune.

The groom gave Rina a crown of flowers, a symbol of his prosperity. She undid the looser of the two belts from her hips and tied it around his solid middle.

Oh, I thought, trying not to look at Torun. That was what giving a belt meant. Oh. And if Bettina had given him his belt, then...

After the ceremony, I tried not to look for him and he did not seek me out. I understood why he made himself scarce. Women gathered in bunches and cast furtive glances at me, while the men stared before turning away. I could ignore it while we ate roast lamb dressed with yogurt and sage. I could forget while Melina, Sarai and Telka danced with me in a circle as the sun went down. But after I returned from putting Telka to bed in Velni-Ani's home, I became conscious of my solitude. I was silent while those around me were dancing, singing, feasting, gossiping.

I heard the roll of Pa's voice. He was telling a story—probably lying, I thought uncharitably. I found him sitting at a table with a loaf of bread stuffed with jam in one hand and his pipe in the other. I did not like his companion at all. In contrast to Pa's easy manner, the stranger seemed, well, twitchy. He was of Pa's height and pale as most Verians. His nose was sharply pointed, his eyes quick, searching. He had a pipe but did not smoke it. He held it before himself and fiddled with it, running his fingers over the stem, along the curve of the bowl, picking at an imagined irregularity of the clay surface. His knee bounced impatiently. The tufts of his fine, thinning hair seemed to be stretching out to possess more than their fair share of space.

"Ah, Lizbet. Heino, this is my eldest daughter."

Heino's eyes darted from my sunburned nose to the dirt under my fingernails.

I nodded at Pa's partner in trade.

"So." He turned to Pa, obviously done with me, and lifted his eyebrows in the direction of Velni-Ani, who was eating stewed apples from a pot. "The old woman's getting tired of life, I hear."

I passed them by. It was better to be alone than to be trapped talking to them.

With the children gone, the dancing had split into pairs. I stood awkwardly in the shadows, just outside the ring of torches bordering the festivities. I watched alone, tapping my feet in an attempt to look like I was just holding back until I learned the steps. I made sure I was on the other side of the clearing from the *hekunaisik*, which leered at the dancers from the place Torun left it. I was so focused on looking interested that I did not see Torun until he nudged me with his elbow.

"I'm learning," I said.

"I can learn you better," he said, forgetful for once about his language. I was so relieved of his company that I forgot about the *hekunaisik*. I decided, also, to ignore what people would say if they saw Torun dancing with me. I was tired of being alone.

My hands went on his forearms, and his on my shoulder blades. At first it was exhilarating, whipping ourselves around in circles, stopping, stomping and changing direction. The speed with which he spun me thrice and gathered me into his arms only to turn me out again made me laugh. Sweat had turned Torun's hair a damp brown, and he was grinning widely.

But the fiddles and drum which sustained us imperceptibly, gradually wound down into a slow, halting rhythm. With the music, the couples left off their wild leaps and settled into closer stances, stepping slowly and near to each other. Near the edge of the dance floor, Torun gathered my arms around his neck and settled his hands around my waist. Step, rock back, step, rock back. Standing so close meant that I could not misstep without crushing Torun's feet, so I spent a good amount of time watching my feet and counting. I leaned into him so that I could better feel where his body would move and how I should match my movements. But I became aware, bit by bit, that his exhalations had turned heavy.

Around us, dancers had begun a ululating song about the brevity of spring. In the third verse, there was a line about the faded leaves underfoot and the chill wind of winter. It was then that Torun broke away from me and strode away into the shadows. Having stood so close and become accustomed to the weight and spread of his hands on my waist and to the strange heat that had unfurled through me, I felt bereft.

I chased after him between the trees, calling his name. He turned, and in the dark, I suppose, it was easier to forget her. He kissed me gently, my first kiss, but the dancing had put me past gentleness. We swayed as we clung to each other and tasted the salt of each other's sweat. He kept one hand on my waist while the other supported my head, but I undid a button of his jacket and put a hand inside to feel his heart beat wildly under the damp, hot shirt. He pulled me closer to him. As our lips broke so that we could breathe, I swear I laughed.

"Lizbet!" Sarai's voice cut through the sounds of revelry. "Where are you?" It was late and *bivin* sisters needed minding.

I pushed Torun away gently, wished him goodnight in his own language and ran off.

"Wait!" he called after me, but I left him there in the shadows. *Mine*, my body sang. *All mine*. I forgot the day's loneliness in the swollen ache of my lips. Velni-Ani's muttering could not touch me. I smiled at Sarai so broadly that her frown faltered. Perhaps I should not care at all that Pa had not sent his message, I thought.

"You come with me," Sarai said, grabbing my hand. "All the women are gathered, so you can't not be here. It would be bad."

In my absence, the composition of the party had changed. Rina and her husband were no longer part of the festivities and most of the men were clustered around the casks of beer and spirit. Sarai led me to where the women had gathered in a circle, holding hands around the fire.

Rina's mother and Velni-Ani held the *hekunaisik* between them. They walked the puppet around the circle as the night before, but now instead of jests and advice, each woman put some sort of curse on its painted face. Some muttered, some spoke loudly.

"False friend."

"Sickness."

"Barren womb."

"Failed harvest."

They stepped past me and turned to Sarai. She looked Velni-Ani in the face, smiled crookedly and said, "Tangled loom."

Melina was last. Her words came out at a whisper. "*Alvinaisik*." And they cast it into the fire.

I felt the gaze of the villagers on me as the flames leapt up. It would be bad if I wasn't there, Sarai had said. This was a sort of test, it had to be. The women began to sing.

Burn hekunaisik, rise into the wind.
Twigs and sticks, take out the sick.
Flames be bold, chase out the cold.
Heat of the fireplace, rise into the wind.

The flames ate through the sacking face and shrivelled the hair of the *hekunaisik*. I kept my face as still as I could as the song continued. I would not be afraid.

Bring them health and bring them wealth
Burn the mist, bring back what's missed
Ashes of a wooden girl, rise into the wind.

The effigy cracked, and a stream of sparks flew up. Someone gave a cheer and the others laughed. The mood returned to that of celebration, but Sarai's hand tightened over mine. "We usually do this at midwinter," she said. "When we need to get rid of our fears."

"So, are you rid of them?" I asked.

Sarai shrugged. "I'm not afraid of anything, so I wouldn't know."

The next morning, the charred remains of the *hekunaisik* had broken down amongst the other burned logs and twigs. Only a shrivelled curl of hay from the *hekunaisik*'s head remained, stuck between two stones that ringed the fireplace. If I hadn't seen the effigy, I would not have known it had ever existed.

On the walk home, everyone was silent and withdrawn. I wanted to tell Torun about the *hekunaisik*, but there was no way of doing so without attracting Melina's attention. She was talking to Pa, conversing about household matters.

Torun looked over his shoulder at me and then he turned back to face the path. And then he stepped more quickly. Why would he not walk next to me? Was it Pa's presence? Or was the *hekunaisik*? Or had the kiss accidentally ruined our friendship? I would have no one else to talk to and then I would need to find a way home. I would ford the river and walk west. I would knock on Ma's door and fling myself into her waiting arms. I would tend the unicorns with single-minded devotion.

My exaggeration was soon put to the test.

When we arrived at the house, there was a familiar, four-footed, grey-white form nibbling raspberries from the spiky growth that emerged from the eastern wall of the family hedge. I could hear the nervous maaaah-maaaaaah of the sheep on the other side of the hedge. They knew Sida as a force of energetic disruption. Her stillness did not comfort them.

Torun glanced at me despite himself, but, for the moment, I only had eyes for my fawn.

"Sida!"

I felt my father watching me as I ran over. This time, Sida stood patiently as I fussed over her. I stretched my arms around her narrow neck and kissed her elegant face. Torun's herb-poultice seemed to have helped the cuts and scratches. I ran my hands over her pointed ears, checking for mites. She was healthy and she was safe. For now. But she blew her breath uneasily and stamped her hooves. What had happened? Why wasn't she with the herd?

There was a rustle through the hedge. Maro, followed by Dan, lurched into view and then retreated a little. Sida gave a nervous side-step.

"Who is this?" Pa asked in Gersan. As if I would give a more honest answer if Melina did not understand. His voice was plummy, but I saw a flicker of greed in his eyes.

"This is one of my…" I almost said fawns. "This is one of my foals. She's a yearling now. I raised her by bottle when her dam died." I brushed Sida's forelock over her forehead to cover the bud. It was as high as my thumb now, but unbruised and sound. I leaned down, running my hands over Sida's body to make sure her legs were strong and her hooves were healthy.

What was she doing here?

"Strange-looking yearling," my father said, rubbing his eyes. "I could use a horse."

Whatever had happened out there, Sida wasn't safe here, either.

With my right hand, I found an old dried, broken strand of raspberry bramble and picked it up as I stood. Ignoring the million palm-pricks of the bramble's thorns, I ran my left hand along her flank. "Good girl, clever girl," I sang. "This girl is not for riding, is she?"

"Perhaps I could find a horse to breed her with." He stepped towards Sida and me.

I swiftly pressed the bramble into her belly. Surprised at the sting, she reared up with a scream and charged away. I took a few steps to see her round the hedge and head towards Fenlen Forest. She leapt down into the streambed and splashed across the river. The water was only knee high now. I threw away the strand as my family turned to watch Sida disappear.

I clenched my bleeding hand as they turned to stare at me.

"Pa, you scared her!" I felt like crying, far more than I had yesterday when he denied the possibility of sending word to Ma. Sida had come to me for help and I had scared her off. I shuddered. I had been like the unicorn mothers who scare off their yearlings, but I had done it too soon. Too soon and for unnatural reasons. But my relation to Pa was natural, was it not? I swallowed my guilt. "She'll stay away now."

"A yearling? She'll come back." He did not look convinced at my lie, bleary as he was from the night's celebration.

We stared at each other until Melina suggested that we go inside to eat.

My father grunted and pushed through the hedge towards the house.

I stayed where I was, looking down to the river. The water had ebbed; I could see the flat top of the larger rocks in places. It was no longer impossible, I felt with a pang, to go across, to find my way home. After all, Sida could.

"*Heirre.*" Torun was the last one outside.

"Torun…" The questions and worries piled up. What did Sida's appearance mean? What about the *hekunaisik*? "Yesterday, the *hekunaisik*…why did they make me hold it? Why are they scared of me?"

He looked at me askance. "People think that by making a *hekunaisik*, they are protecting the bride or the village. But they are also making it alive, in a way. It takes on their fears." He turned my face carefully toward his and I met his eyes. Before, Torun had said that there was no human magic. I was beginning to understand why he stuck so firmly to that belief. "But you are strong. You are not a *hekunaisik*. And Sida understands you. She came back."

For a moment, I thought he would kiss me. His eyelashes were tipped with gold.

"I just wished she hadn't *today*."

"Like you, she wanders on her own time."

"Torun! LIZBET! COME!" Sarai's sharp voice sounded no softer from far away.

We made our way slowly to the hedge. Torun lifted a bough to let us through. As I walked into the green shadows, he swiftly ducked and kissed me. He might have aimed for my mouth, but I was so surprised by his movement that I stumbled and he kissed me instead under my left ear as I tripped into the yard.

"There you are!" Sarai lectured from the portico. "If this is what being a mother is like, I never want children. Now get inside so I don't have to deal with everything myself!"

If Torun was red in the face and I was bashful, we were fortunate that the family was distracted. Unfortunately, they were distracted by Sida's appearance and what it might mean. Telka was telling Melina that Sida was like her unicorn toy.

"I want to see the *uksarv* again," she said

"Not *uksarv*," I explained in Verian. What was the word I wanted? "It's an *ufoli* horse."

"But it had fluffy hair like the toy Torun carved me. You said my toy was an *uksarv*," Telka said. "And you told Sarai you saw *uksarv* when you and Torun went exploring. Sarai, don't kick me!"

My father cleared his throat. Telka stopped whining and Sarai, it seemed, stopped kicking.

"Telka. Clever girl. Why don't you show everyone what you told me about?"

Telka's expression changed from the open-mouthed dismay of betrayal to narrow-eyed judgment of me, Torun and Sarai. She bounced up from her seat and went to our sleeping nook.

"She's going to show you that toy Torun carved her," Sarai said. "She's always making things up."

But Sarai was wrong. Telka trotted back to us with her treasure behind her back. With her chin in the air, she presented to us the alicorn I had stowed away in my bag.

"Where did you get that?" Sarai said, her eyes going from Telka to me.

"She snooped," Torun added. "Telka!"

"So, you knew as well," Pa said with a smile.

Torun fell silent.

"I need to find her, my *uksarv*, so I can go home," I said. "There's something…off…about the forest and I can't go into it without her."

"You're not going to share your treasure with us, you mean?"

"What treasure? You…you think that's worth anything?" It had value, but I wasn't sure what he expected from it. Ma had managed to build a life not much better than the one he had.

"I'll find out," Pa said smoothly. "I'll go into the city and figure out exactly how much it's worth. And in the meantime, you'll find your little pet and bring her here."

"Yes," Telka said. "Please!"

"I'll…I'll stay here. I'll stay indoors. I'll learn to weave."

"Pfft." That was from Sarai. She knew me better.

"Then your pet will come to you." Pa tossed the alicorn from hand to hand. "I can wait."

"I suppose you'll have to," I shot back.

He smiled.

Sarai rolled her eyes.

That night, the gap between me, Telka and Sarai in the big bed seemed to have mysteriously disappeared.

That made it more difficult to sneak out once everyone had fallen asleep.

CHAPTER FIFTEEN

Forest Society

I awoke at dawn and packed my things—this time, I took my boots and my oilskin. I nabbed a few links of sausage from the beams and a small bag of oats. The alicorn was still with Pa.

"Lizbet?" Telka watched me from behind the curtain.

"I'm going to find the *uksarv*," I whispered. She could explain to Pa how she saw fit. Sida had come for me and I needed to know why.

Torun was dozing in the lambing shed. He sat up when he heard me leap down from the trap door. He combed the hay out of his hair with his fingers and lit a small lantern. He shaded its light with his other hand. As he climbed over the fence, I wondered whether we should kiss again and we lurched towards each other indecisively. Our heads smacked together.

"Agh!" I said, and then while I giggled, he kissed me. Holding hands, we snuck out of the family enclosure and made our way down to the riverbank where we could talk. The grass was cold and wet with dew and made slithering sounds as we went.

"It is a mess," he said.

True. But which mess was he talking about?

"We do not know the *uksarv* and now he wants us to control them."

Ah, that mess. "As long as he thinks there's only one."

Torun nodded. "What are you going to do?"

"Stay home?"

"Learn to weave?"

We laughed at the thought. I'd find Sida, but I would *not* tell Pa. I did not like the idea of Pa getting mixed up with the *uksarv*. It bothered me in a way that Ma's business never had.

Torun broke my thoughts with another kiss. "You could stay up at the high pasture. With me. I'll be up until it's time to shear them. Don't go into Fenlen Forest. Please."

"Why not? If I find a way home, I should probably go."

"You should?"

The question caught me off guard. Of course, I should. I couldn't abandon Ma. I needed to at least *try* to find my way home. What was keeping me here? At first it had been Sida. And the fear of getting lost in a forest I thought I knew. But now...

"Don't go, please." He cleared his throat. "You know I don't believe in nonsense stories. But the forest is dangerous."

The sun was coming up, warm on our backs. The shadows were fleeing west towards the forest. I rebelled against Torun's words and against my own fears. It was a strange place, perhaps, but it had never threatened me.

"The forest's not dangerous!" Torun himself didn't believe the stories. I kissed the corner of his right eye. "Why don't you come with me and you'll find out? Maybe we'll run away together."

The corners of his mouth tugged down for a moment. "I am not funny." He huffed at his ungrammatical Gersan. "I am not *being* funny. *This* is not funny. People are lost there."

Ah. That was what had happened. "Did she...did she go missing looking for a lamb? A hawk had snatched it?" But even as I said it, I knew it didn't make sense. If Bettina was lost that night, how could she have woven my unicorn hairs into Torun's belt?

His eyes narrowed, surprised and just a bit suspicious. "No," he said. "If Telka told you, she's making up stories. *That* was a year before it happened." I waited for more, but he fell silent.

Torun made it sound like her disappearance wasn't caused by the forest and he didn't believe in fairy folk such as the Alvina. Then why was he scared?

He was staring across the river at the dim shapes of the boulders.

I wanted him to look at *me*. "But the forest isn't so bad. Look at my father...*he* made it across! And if you're with me, you'll be safe. I've been there lots of times. There isn't a border that you cross and poof! you're lost."

His pale skin flushed to match the rash of pimples across his right cheek. His chin pushed out slightly. "Maybe the border is in myself."

"But you'd be with me!" Didn't that make a difference? Torun pulled his spine straight, reaching his full height. As if he needed to show physical strength to oppose me. "Maybe I am weak to stay, maybe strong. But I cannot go there. I won't."

"Fine." Suddenly, we were too serious. It was as if he were no longer having an argument with me, but with someone else.

"Yes. Fine. Do not go to the cave."

"I wasn't going to."

I shouldered my bag and stalked away across the uneven stones of the riverbank, sloshing through the water. I should have wished him a pleasant time with the herd, but I was rankled by the ghost that had turned my proposed adventure into a tussle of wills.

On the far bank, I looked over my shoulder. Torun was walking away with his shoulders hunched. I could see the path of flattened grass ahead of him, the river, the cluster of trees I now knew as Melina's home. The landscape now held meaning for me. Yet, ahead of me, the incline of the escarpment beckoned. The striations of rock were shot through by veins of plant life. Somewhere, there was a trail.

I turned west and made my way through the scattered boulders and the scrub of bilberry bushes. Torun's boulder was still there, with the moss growing stealthily across the carved face. Moss didn't usually grow so fast, I thought with a twinge of unease. To the left and south of Torun's boulder, a faint path, a thin, hard-packed dirt line among the grass, led along the base of the ravine before forking off. One line led further south, where the wind brought a faint, sulphuric stink. To the cave, I knew. The other path was marked more by an absence of trees and bushes than any indent in the grass and weeds. It was a path visible only to someone looking for a way and it led me up a gradual incline that switched back and forth to the top of the ravine. How long the trail had existed, I could not know.

I pulled myself up the steep path, singing the song from Rina's wedding to calm my nerves. *Blow away the dust, good wind, blow away the dust. With my heart's old sorrow, take it to the dusk…* Whereas it had once been slippery with ice and slush, the incline was now tufted with new growth, with bushy trees. And as I scrambled up, among the old, thick-trunked trees, I felt pressure building on my ears, like they had filled with water. The aspens and larches were fringed with shadows. *The forest's not dangerous. If you're with me, you'll be safe.* That was what I told Torun. And now I suspected—no, I knew—that I had been wrong.

Before, I had lived in Fenlen Forest. It had been my home. The only habitat I had known. But now I had been in another forest. On the other side of the river, the shadows matched the overlapping pattern of the leaves above. In Torun's forest, the silence was cut through with the baaing of sheep or the chitter of squirrels fighting in the canopy.

Now I had returned to the forest, going west instead of east, and everything seemed strange. I could see that the shadows clung to each stipple in the trees' bark, each dimple of the leaves, each sap-filled vein that strained out from the skin of the plant stalks. In the silence, the pipit's cheep seemed higher and sweeter and the woodlark's song carried an echo. But the tension in my ears built, like I was diving deeper and deeper into a lake.

"Sida?" Unlike the birds' calls, my voice did not soar; it curled into the soft, thick moss and lay still there. I opened my mouth to call again, and then closed it.

The pressure on my ears began to hurt; I had been gone too long.

I knelt into the loam and ran my hands under fallen leaves. The leaves were warm and dry, but the earth underneath was cool and damp.

What right did I have to be here? What had given me the right, for so many years? The forest had been mine, I had believed, but perhaps I had equally belonged to it. I had given something in return. My Pa. And Pa had sacrificed us for the right to walk through the forest without harm.

For years, I had taken things from the forest. Alicorn, yes, but also flowers, wood for the fire, pebbles that felt nice in the palm of my hand and that made satisfying plonking noises when tossed in a creek. And what had I given, since the hurt of Pa's absence had waned?

What was I willing to give for Sida? For the forest?

I swallowed, uncomfortable with the thought. Pa had been my blood and now I had nothing, I thought as I took my hand out from under the leaves. I looked through my bag, knowing there was little in it that the forest would value. My waterskin. A small bag of oats. Flint and tinder. My hand passed over my knife. That was something, I thought. I unsheathed it.

Holding the knife in my right hand, I pricked the fingertips of my left hand and placed my hand to the earth once more. I pressed down and felt the soil give up its moisture, felt the water cling to the grooves of my fingerprints as my blood oozed out. The earth felt warm now, I thought, warm as flesh. I took my hand away and licked my fingers. The tang of blood mixed with the rich taste of the soil.

"Sida?" I called and the pressure on my ears gave way. My voice carried through the trees, high and hopeful as the bird-song. But I shivered, because now I knew that I was only a guest. With my right hand, I unscrewed the jar of alicorn and dabbed a finger into the white ointment. I touched each of the five cuts. They stung, itched, scabbed over. A few seconds later, I knew, the scabs would flake away.

That first day I did not dare to lose sight of the ridge. I did not believe that I would find Sida. Unicorns take their dignity very seriously, and I had insulted her. I had welcomed her presence with a thorny raspberry bramble. I should not have done it, part of me said. But with Pa standing there, it had been the only thing to do. I followed the ridge in a straight line north, pretending that I did not feel lonely.

But in the evening, as I was looking down from the ridge, I spotted the herd of *uksarv*. In the honey-light of the afternoon, their edges seemed to fade into the rising mist. They were standing in the riverbed, ambling through and dipping their heads to drink as they crossed over to my side. Towards me! My pulse throbbed. Where was Sida?

There. At the edge of the herd. She was back with them, now that I had chased her away. But not quite. She lagged behind. I was so focused on her, on the proud toss of her head that told of her secret dejection, that I didn't realize that part of the herd had disappeared. But there were fewer of them now. Only the does heavy in their pregnancy remained, picking their way up towards the escarpment by a path I had not seen before. Where had the others gone?

A nicker answered my thoughts. I turned, and there was the

scarred matriarch with her milky eye. Behind her, a group of does cropped at the low-hanging leaves. None of them had the low-slung bellies of pregnancy. Those does were rejoining the group one by one on the path. And then came Sida. The speckled second-in-command was nowhere to be seen.

Sida circled the perimeter of the group, but the does turned away from her, forming a circle with the pregnant ones in the middle. Only the matriarch remained outside the circle, watching me.

Sida frisked in the matriarch's direction, followed the gaze of her good eye and spotted me watching from behind an ash. She came to me.

I put out my hand and she snuffled at it. I fumbled with my pack and offered her my oats, but she did not want them. Instead, Sida knelt down and looked at me. She turned her neck to look at the matriarch and then at her back. She wanted me to get up onto her back.

The matriarch looked on impassively.

"You're too young," I said to Sida, but I was secretly pleased. If she wanted me to climb up on her back, she wanted me to stay with her. Gently, I swung my leg over her, and she rose up, struggling a little at first, because of the odd sensation of having weight on her.

I clutched at her mane as she stood, rump first and then lifting her forelegs. Well, it was as new to her as it was to me. I gripped tight as she started off at a brisk walk. We went south, a direction I had not been in, where the ground sloped gently. We must be going over the *Alvina birlan*, I thought.

The escarpment began to lower, but Sida stopped at an overhang that dipped gently down on the left.

Below us, I saw a small group of *uksarv*.

I recognized the barrel-chested buck. He was standing watch: ears alert, tail switching back and forth. Behind him was the heavily pregnant doe with the speckled face I had encountered earlier. The matriarch's second-in-command. She had lost her horn and was lying on the forest floor with her legs tucked under her. She looked tired, resigned. She was very close to giving birth. Around her were three other does, some visibly expecting, but none so far along as this one. They seemed to be trying to comfort her, but to no avail.

"He must be building a herd," I said to myself. "Stealing does away from another group." I looked at Sida, at the fixed set of her ears. That must have been what was happening. He must have found her and has been trying to add her to his... whatever it was.

But now what, I thought to myself. Evidently, I didn't think fast enough for her because Sida backed up and ducked her neck down. I tumbled over her shoulders and found myself sitting hard in the undergrowth.

The old buck raised his head and looked left and right, trying to see what might dare encroach on his territory.

And Sida was nowhere I could see her. No, I *did* see her. She was moving quietly to the south and west from me.

I took one step and a stick cracked underfoot.

A snort and the shuffle of leaves underfoot told me the buck had heard me and was coming to investigate. Somehow, he had missed Sida's progress.

Now I knew what Sida wanted to do. She was going to rescue the pregnant doe by instigating a raiding party. I was the bait, she was the escape artist.

I had succeeded in distracting the old buck. He saw me and stopped, turning his head to consider me with rolling eyes. I didn't kneel. My plan was to climb a tree if I needed to.

I needed to keep my eyes on him. If my eyes went to Sida, he would look.

He lowered his horn.

I backed up into the pricking branches of a pine. He began slinking forward, snaking his neck to the left and right.

When I hit the trunk of the pine, I pivoted on my heel and scaled the first three branches. Now that the buck was focused on me, I could spare a glance at Sida.

She nudged the doe to get up. The doe was tired and gave a shake of her head.

I threw a pinecone at the buck and instantly regretted it when the buck charged at the tree. He reared up and stretched out his neck to bite me. I scaled the next branch, and regret aside, threw another pinecone. He squealed in anger.

Below, Sida stretched out her neck and nipped at the doe's haunches. The doe gave an irritated whinny as she stood up quickly. Sida gave a bugling cry. Perhaps it was triumphant. I thought it was a bad idea.

The buck turned to protect his does. He and Sida circled each other, pranced forward, darted back.

But each was intent on getting the other away from the does, which meant the fight was near the speckled one. Whenever Sida tried something to urge the doe up the hill, the barrel-chested buck circled around and blocked their way.

Sida reared in aggravation and cried out again, as if she was calling someone. Me?

I scrambled down the tree.

The old buck turned, looked over his shoulders and aimed a kick at Sida. She leapt away, but his hoof landed close to the doe's round belly, on her haunch. She fell over and then heavily got to her feet.

I gasped and threw another pinecone at the buck, then searched for a rock.

And then the matriarch arrived, distracting the buck with

a stern call of challenge. Sida, head down, stubby horn pointed, pushed the buck farther south, rearing and bucking.

With the buck fighting off the matriarch, I clambered down the incline and ran to the little group.

Sida and I stood on either side of the specked doe and quickly led her away towards the rest of her herd. The others could choose to stay or follow as they wished. The sounds of the *uksarv* duel escalated and then faded as we made our way north.

The speckled doe walked slowly. The kick to her side had been a hard one, and there was a curve of broken skin. Her tightly stretched belly rippled as the fawn inside shifted its position. I saw something—a knee? a hoof?—pushing at the doe's skin from within. I ran my hand over the doe's stomach, feeling uneasy. The fall could not have been safe for either mother or fawn.

When we reached the matriarch's herd, the does surrounded the speckled one and Sida and me, nosing us curiously. They began moving away as a group.

Somewhere behind us, the buck bellowed. The does burst into flight. They first ran forward, leaving the three of us behind. Then they circled back and roiled around Sida and the speckled doe. This time, they stayed tightly around the doe, but Sida slid out of the group.

She trotted up to me and butted me in the shoulder with the ridge of her nose. I stumbled back, and she nibbled at my hair to apologize. And then she butted me again. It was time to go home, she was telling me, because I had no business here.

She turned and galloped after the herd.

I climbed down the face of the ravine before the buck saw me.

CHAPTER SIXTEEN

New Arrival

The forest's not dangerous! Ha. Now I knew it might welcome me, or not.

And then there were the *uksarv*. I had once thought that unicorns were solitary creatures, wise and withdrawn. That they were beyond the flaws of humans and the appetites of animals. Maybe they still were, closer to home. Here they weren't.

I wasn't going to go after them or look for my path in the dark. Not when the buck was roaming around in a temper. At the base of the escarpment, I tripped over an *uksarv* horn. I almost tucked it into my bag and, thinking better of it, threw it into the scrubby bushes. I wasn't risking Pa picking through my things.

I went back to the house in the gloaming.

Pa was on the portico, packing up. I didn't understand. He had just come back—Melina and Sarai had not woven enough for him to go out yet.

"Any luck?" he said.

"Pa," I said. "Give me my horn."

"No. I'm going to meet Heino and we're going to sell it."

"It's not yours."

"I don't believe you understand how a family business works." He smoothed his moustache with his thumb and forefinger. "You see, you make things or find things and I sell them. I'll give you a percentage of the profit. Like I give Sarai for her weaving."

During the clamour of supper, I tried to steal it back from him, so he resorted to tucking it under his shirt.

When he left the next morning, he said, "I wonder, do you have to saw the horn off? Does it regrow or do you have to kill the beast first?"

"That's horrible!" I exclaimed.

"Thank you," he said, with a wink that I did not like at all.

That day, I stayed and weeded the vegetable patch with Dan. I chopped wood with Maro. I went inside and started the process of learning to spin on a drop spindle with Telka.

"Go away," Sarai said after our midday meal. "You are trying, but I can't work with you sighing over your yarn all the time."

"Do you need vegetables? Wood?" I said.

"Go to the forest, you *bivin naisik*," Sarai said, folding her arms. "I don't care what you do, but don't stay in here, getting in the way. You make my fingers itch." That was what she always said two seconds before she pinched people. There was nothing spiteful in her words, but there was only so much space for near-grown girls in the house. Sarai knew she belonged inside. I belonged outside.

I went to Maro and Dan. "Vegetables? Wood?"

But they had their own confederacy of two and they didn't want me either.

And, in truth, Sarai was right. I had been sighing and getting in the way. I went back to Fenlen Forest, but cautiously. Each day I had walked a little further, learning to recognize the shape of certain trunks, the awkward slump of a broken branch. When I lived with Ma, I had grown familiar with the paths near our house over years, not months. I had once trusted the unicorns with my safety, but now I was alone.

The first day, I was relieved not to see unicorns. But it was a selfish sort of relief. If I did not see them, I could not disobey my inclinations or my father's wishes. But by the second day, I worried about Sida and the speckled doe. Had Sida been accepted? Had the fawn been born? But I could not find them and could not know. And so, I looked for distraction.

On the third day, I ranged north along the ravine face. I slid down the slope, forded the river and found the sheep path.

When I reached the high pasture, I saw Torun sitting with his face lifted to the sun and his eyes closed, thinking. The setting sun cast his shadow long on the grass.

I decided to play a small trick that would shake him from his reverie. I snuck up behind him and placed my cold fingertip against the nape of his neck where the fine, blond hair thickened. I thought he would jump. Instead, he leaned back and caught my arms. He kissed my hands, dirty as they were, and then my wrists.

I laughed and he pulled me down beside him into the grass. "You were bored?"

I kissed the tip of his nose. He considered my aim to be off. What is learning to kiss like? A little sloppy, a little animal, but hugely exciting. And yet. And yet, while we kissed, the thoughts crept in. I kept thinking about secrets, about who shared them, who told them, who benefited from them.

"We can't tell anyone," I said sometime later, as I caught my breath. "About this."

"Your father would be... *zastola*." Most terrible.

If they knew, Pa would have a way to make me do what he wanted. I wasn't quite sure how he'd use the knowledge, but he would. Melina would be...I had no idea, but she would not be happy. I did not see how Torun and I could kiss except in secret. Unless we weren't here at all. When we kissed, it was like we were disappearing from the world around us. Like the *uksarv* vanishing in the mist. But it was too fast and, like watching the vanishing *uksarv*, kissing Torun was something I hadn't had time to understand.

I sat up and told Torun what I had seen: the herd's strange migration up the escarpment, the buck, Sida's rescue. "There's something strange about how they move," I said. "Like they disappear or something. I don't understand it."

"Some animals move very quietly. But tell me about the does." What seemed to interest him most was not the disappearing act, but the idea that the *uksarv* went to the forest to give birth, though they seemed to graze on both sides of the river. "I have heard that some kinds of fish go back to the place where they were hatched when they spawn. I wonder if this is the same."

His curiosity was pushing against his sense of duty and rootedness and his fear of the forest. The forest might be dangerous, but its risks seemed more logical to me than the village, with the villagers' fear of the Alvina and the *hekunaisik*.

"Come with me and maybe we'll find out."

He lifted his eyebrows and grinned. "You? You did not like sheep giving birth. What about *bleeuch*?"

"The doe that Sida saved...I'm worried about her," I admitted.

The teasing expression subsided from Torun's face. "Why?"

"The buck kicked her hard and she's close to giving birth."

"Do...do you know where she is?" He knew enough to be worried and that made my heart knot.

But I didn't.

For the next three days, I went looking for the herd, though my desire for Torun made returning to the forest difficult. When I came to the ravine, I felt a pull away from Fenlen Forest, towards him. And the air would weigh heavily on my ears until I cut my fingers and bled into the earth. I felt that I was cheating, that I was giving my blood too lightly.

I worried that my thoughts, which haunted me as I ran along the deer paths, kept the unicorns away. In the afternoons, I went up to Torun.

And on the fourth day, Sida was there, pacing back and forth in front of him in the high pasture. I was struck by the force with which she raked the ground with her hooves, by the muscles strong under her coat. She had grown stronger and faster than I wanted to believe.

"What does she want?" he asked.

"She wants us to go with her." I remembered the does in the forest. "They need help."

We gathered up his kit, his water cauldron, a lantern. Sida circled around us as we made our preparations.

"How are we going to get this to the forest? What about the sheep?"

Sida gave a little rear and pawed the ground. Then she knelt.

I swung my leg over her back and twined my fingers in her mane.

"Come on, Sida," I said. But Sida arched her neck back to give me a scolding look. She waited for Torun to climb behind me with his arms around my waist.

Sida stood, and as she stepped forward, I felt none of the hesitation I had sensed in my earlier ride.

The ride down the valley, across the river and up the escarpment was a dark, nervous blur. We had little idea of where we were, only that time seemed to race with us. We soon saw the gold haze of the *uksarv* in the forest around us, coalescing around the doe in labour.

The doe made hoarse, wounded sounds. She lay down and rolled back and forth and then rested on her side. Her lungs heaved and heaved with pain. And the fawn would not come.

Sida halted and we slid down. Torun ran over and knelt at

the speckled doe's side. After a brief, assessing glance under her tail, he ran his hands over her, put his ear to her side.

"There is still a heartbeat," he said, beckoning me. He put his arm around my shoulders and guided me to the doe's swollen side. At first, I could only hear her steady beat, strong and fast because of her travail. And then, running above it was a flickering pit-pit-pit-pit.

"She'll be safe?" I asked, relieved.

He ran his hands along her side. "As safe as she could be. Build a fire." Torun's voice was not happy. "I'll get water," he said.

It was only after I coaxed a flame into being that I realized that "as safe as she could be" did not really promise safety at all.

It was horrible, feeding the fire, heating water in our cauldron while the speckled doe moaned. Sida touched her nose to the crease between the doe's neck and chin. The doe nipped at her, exhausted and scared.

When the water was hot, Torun shrugged off his vest and untied the belt around his waist. He lifted the shirt over his shoulders and tossed it onto the rest of his discarded clothes. He soaped his hands and forearms and washed in the hot water.

"You had better wash, too," he said. This was not a time for squeamishness, his tone told me. I rolled up my sleeves.

By the weak light of the lantern, Torun announced that the doe's body was ready, but that nothing was coming out. "Go and see if you can comfort her. Talk to her." He went down by the doe's tail. I went to her head.

I had no idea what to do.

But then the doe gave a shrill cry and thrashed. I looked over at her hindquarters.

"*Yimma naisik*," Torun crooned, but he stood up and stepped back. "Lizbet, please come here." We squatted down together and he pointed without touching. "See that? It's the rump and

tail. The *uksarv voon* has turned around. Its legs are tucked in and
we need to shift them around," he said. "But she doesn't want my
help. She doesn't trust me. I need you. You'll have to reach in with
your arm. You need to find the back feet and pull them out. The
contractions are going to be strong, but unless the feet come out
first, the *uksarv voon* will be stuck. Are you ready?"

"No." But I leaned over by her tail anyway. I put my hand
into the tight, damp, muscular cave before the contraction came
and squeezed down on my arm. I gave a stifled moan of my own,
a faint echo of the doe's pain, until it eased, and then I reached
further.

"Got it," I said, my fingers closing on two tiny hooves. There
was something wrong, though, an angle that did not fit. I grunted
along with the doe this time. "I think there's something wrong
with the fawn's leg. It's bent," I said through clenched teeth.

"Straighten it," Torun said. "Bring it towards the outside."

It was hard work. The fawn, inside, recoiled at first from my
attempt to pull its legs straight, but I was stronger. Slowly, the
angle unbent itself and I eased out two bloody, cloven hooves. I
grunted with the effort.

"Don't let go," Torun said behind me. "When she pushes,
you pull the baby *uksarv* out. Ready?" he said. "Pull. NOW." I
pulled, and then Torun put his arms around mine, gripped
and pulled with me as the doe pushed her best. Pull, pause.
Pull, pause.

It seemed like eternity had passed before the long legs
emerged, then the rump and ribcage. I adjusted my grip as the
doe kicked in the effort to pass the fawn's shoulders through,
inch by inch. The shoulders were the biggest and the rest slithered out onto Torun and me.

I had a glimpse of the nose and closed eyes before Torun
pushed me aside and took the membrane off the fawn's face,

cleared its nostrils and mouth of mucus. It had kicked and pulled away from me in the womb, but had it survived its passage into the world?

Next to us, the doe, panting and exhausted, struggled to deliver the afterbirth.

The fawn lay there, limp, as Torun breathed into its mouth. He pushed on its chest. Another breath. He sat back on his heels and wiped his face in the crook of his elbow.

We looked at the small, still thing. It coughed.

The doe lay with her head on the ground, so we dried the fawn off as best we could with my shirt and set it next to her teats. Sida nuzzled the doe, and I went to stroke her neck. The doe stood up slowly, gingerly and looked back and down at her fawn.

Below her, the fawn struggled to its feet and stretched out its neck to suckle. It sat down quickly, as if its tender bones had been bruised. I stepped forward to help the fawn up, but another doe from the herd nudged me aside. She also had no horn and her own sturdy fawn trotted close by her heels. This doe placed her nose expertly under the new fawn's frail forelegs and supported it while it drank.

Torun brushed the outside of my hand with one finger, a reminder that we had other work to do. We tipped the cauldron over the fire and stamped out the embers. Only after the hiss of hot wood had faded did I realize that we should have washed our hands again in the warm water. Instead, we gathered our things and stumbled down to the riverside, dirty and exhausted. I went first, stripping off my clothing as I stood knee deep in the water.

It was dark. It didn't matter if he saw me or not. My shirt was full of blood and mucous and feces and I didn't want it on me anymore. I squatted down in the cold, running stream and then lay down.

"They will see your hair is wet," he said.

"Don't care." I scrubbed my clothes but knew they would still be mucky. I tossed them onto the stones.

"You should take my shirt," he said.

There wasn't any reason to say anything else. I sloshed out to him, and he held the shirt out in front of him like a flag of surrender.

I climbed into it while, a few safe paces away, he peeled off his trousers.

"Stay," he said.

I watched him, a dim glowing slip of white in the river. He had a long walk back to the high pasture. I hoped nothing had happened to the sheep.

"I wasn't scared," I said. My voice was sudden and loud in the night.

He splashed water onto himself. "I did not say you were." He was scrubbing at his arms with handfuls of rocky sand. "But I was. It was close."

And now I felt foolish.

But he passed over my bravado. "You were strong. You did well." He walked out of the river, wet and shivering and weary.

I went over to embrace him. Because I saw that he needed comfort, and I did too. His wet back was stippled with goose-bumps. I rubbed my cheek against his chest.

I no longer felt the cold. Instead, I was filled with excitement and dread shot through with exhaustion. I needed to do something or say something, or I would burst.

"Thank you for coming with me." I said at the very same time as he said, "Your nose is freezing." We lapsed into silence. It was such an odd, everyday thing for him to say, but I was grateful for it. I pressed my cold nose into his shoulder and he laughed.

A splish-splash and whinny announced Sida's arrival. Holding one another, we watched her approach. But then there was a strange cry, like some night bird. Instead of drawing closer together, we stepped apart.

When she reached us, Sida nudged at me and I scratched her neck. Torun turned to struggle into his trousers and vest, slinging his belt around his neck like a scarf. "I have a long walk." He drew his fingers through her mane.

Sida stood quite still for a moment, took two steps to the left and vanished with Torun. I blinked. When I had first told him about the unicorns' ability to disappear, he hadn't believed. But now, I ran forward to the spot I had last seen them and couldn't find anything. I was too tired to think it through.

I picked up my wet clothes with my fingertips and started walking back in Torun's shirt. I had planned to hang the clothing up on the portico, but I simply walked through the house and dropped them on the floor before I collapsed into the big bed. I dreamt of nothing, of the darkness.

CHAPTER SEVENTEEN

Bettina

"Pfft."

I opened my eyes reluctantly. Sarai had drawn the curtain and beyond her, the open windows let in the bright sunshine. Out of sight, the clackety-clack told me that Melina was weaving at the big loom. Telka was humming and spinning.

"So, you're alive."

Sarai picked up my damp breeches and then my equally damp shirt. She frowned, seeing a third heap on the floor. She picked it up. She rubbed the cloth between her thumb and forefinger, noting the rougher weave. Frowning, she held it at arm's length, to confirm what she already knew. Sarai knew her own handiwork, the difference between cloth made for men's work in the field and women's work indoors. She knew that it wasn't my shirt, that it was Torun's shirt.

Sarai looked over at me. Her forehead wrinkled.

I didn't say anything. How could I? I didn't have the words to explain what had happened.

She looked over her shoulder in the direction of her mother and sister and tossed the shirt at me. I caught it in one hand.

"Take that out of here," she hissed and she turned out of the nook, letting the curtain drop.

I dressed in a clean shift and skirt and bundled Torun's shirt into a ball. Where was my pack? I must have left it with the herd last night. What else had we left there? I was going to have to go back for it.

Sarai was on the portico, laying out my breeches to dry. She opened my damp shirt and made a sound of disgust.

"What have you been doing?" Despite my efforts, the shirt was stained with rusty smears. It was going to have to be washed.

"Hurt animal. Torun helped me."

"Hmm. Sure." And then Sarai gave me that same worried look, which was so unlike her. "Just don't...Lizbet, be gentle."

What did that mean? I stared at her and she rolled her eyes. "And don't be stupid."

The summer morning was warm on the high pasture and the sheep grazed or huddled against each other. Torun was wearing his spare shirt and training his dogs, teaching them to lie down in the grass and crawl forward on their bellies while his arm was outstretched and his hand was flat. With a turn up of his hand, the dogs leapt up and raced towards him.

"Torun!"

The dogs flew towards me, eager to say hello, but with a whistle, Torun called them to his side.

"What happened?" I threw him his shirt and he spread it out on the grass.

"Nothing."

"You disappeared. With Sida."

He shook his head. "It was like I blinked and...and it was early in the afternoon. She was with me and we walked back to the high pasture and the flock."

"So?"

"So, I got there just in time to see us leave."

We stared at each other.

Sida had not just disappeared. She had also moved back through the day. She had moved through time. With Torun.

"Then there *is* magic," I said.

"I said there's no human magic," Torun said, trying to limit the impossible. "This is the nature of the *uksarv*."

I thought of Pa, of my lost years, of Bettina from years past. Perhaps there was some key to all this. "If we watch them, maybe we can understand."

"Maybe," he said, but he did not seem particularly interested in following the herd. He leaned forward to kiss me, beginning light and teasing, on my eyelids, the tip of my nose, then my mouth. I searched for places to impress my memory onto his skin, the dip of his collarbone, the soft skin inside his upper arm, behind his sunburned ears.

I might have bitten him on the shoulder and soon we were engaged in a sort of cooperative wrestling with our clothes mostly on. Though a shift and a skirt, I thought, were not much.

He put his hand tentatively on the inside of my leg, just above my knee where my shift had ridden up. I put my hand over his, unsure whether I wanted to slide it up, or to place it somewhere safer, like my waist, his waist, the grass. Or perhaps his hand was where it belonged right now.

We kissed and our fingers twined. For a moment, I almost forgot everything around us. But Torun's refusal to know, to recognize the strangeness of the *uksarv* and the world pressed in on my mind.

"You could come with me," I said. "I have to fetch your cauldron back for you. Come with me. You went into the forest and you came out safely."

"I was with you because we had work to do," he said simply. "And now you are here and I am not in the forest. I do not have to be there to be with you."

"But…"

"I will bring the sheep down for shearing soon," he said. "But I cannot leave them. They must be washed and shaved. I will have to teach Maro and Dan."

The sheep were his work. The unicorns were mine. My work had once tied me to Ma, and I had been cut loose. But Torun was still tied to his home.

I ached to run back to him as I walked down. At the river, I paused to smooth my shift, to retie my belt around my skirt. Except for the belt, these were not my clothes. They were not mine. Was he? Had she kissed him behind his ear, or did that place belong exclusively to me? Had he admired the curve of her ankles in the palms of his hands? How did a person ask those questions without being consumed with possessive hunger? And there were other questions. What had happened to her?

Torun's dislike of the forest and Melina's curse on the *hekun-aisik* suggested something strange. Did it have to do with magic or something else? I sang as I climbed. *Blow away the dust, good wind, blow away the dust. With my heart's old sorrow...* Was the song about someone free to walk away from sorrow? Or did they carry it everywhere they went?

In Fenlen, I found the cauldron and my pack where we had left them. Last night, I had stamped out the fireplace, poured water over the embers and kicked some dirt over it, but this morning there was already a bunch of new fern heads unfurling in the spot.

The herd was nearby—it had drifted further west to a soft, grassy patch. I saw the speckled doe and the fawn sleeping between its mother's legs. It looked frail, but alive. When I tried to draw close, the matriarch met me and stood firmly in my way. I had done my part, but the herd was not welcoming visitors.

Sida emerged from the group of does and trotted along behind me. Her companionship was a consolation for being sent away. She came down the escarpment with me. We were near the fork in the paths, near the place I had met Torun.

I turned to pat her, hold her, to scratch her in the places she liked.

"My baby," I said. "What mischief you've been up to! How did you vanish yesterday, just like that?"

She stepped back and stood perfectly still, except for her ears, which twitched back and forth. She seemed to be thinking. Suddenly, around her, the leaves shrank into buds, the grass withdrew into the ground, which became cold and hard underfoot. With a rustle of wind, the fallen leaves lifted back onto the trees, turning from brown to red to gold.

Autumn.

I remembered that first day I had explored with Torun, the girl's scream. Had it been mine? Or someone else's? I ran forward towards Sida and she remained where she was, as if she were concentrating very hard. When I stood beside her and looked around, I saw the leaves and grass turning from life to death all around me.

And now I heard the sobbing. It was hushed, bitten back.

Stepping cautiously, I approached the sound. Sida followed me, kicking up the leaves.

There, where I had first met Torun, a girl stood with her head pressed on the boulder. Her elbows were propped on the rock above and she seemed to be pulling at her own hair.

"Bettina," I said.

She lifted her face fast. She was silent, suspicious of having her feelings seen.

She had a bit more of her mother in her, a slight fineness to her features. Her chin was more pointed, her throat slimmer. Perhaps she was just hungrier. She was not quite a mirror image: a refraction, not a reflection of who I might be.

"Are you...are you all right?"

Her eyes went big. I put my hand out to her.

She screamed. Not with fright alone, but with rage. She stooped down and picked up a rock.

Now I pivoted on my heel and ran. The rock went wide, flickering through the bushes and falling on my right.

I saw Sida standing, watching me with her head cocked to the right. She turned as I neared her. I put my hand on her shoulder, and around us, the days blurred as the world cooled and warmed and then settled as we found the heat of summer.

Despite the heat, I was shivering. Sida nibbled on a patch of bilberries, but I sat down among the low-lying shrubs that grew in carpets around the boulders between the river and the escarpment.

I had seen her. She had seen me. And between us there was a year in which she disappeared.

What had happened to her? I had found her, if just for a few moments. If I had done it once, could I do it again? And if I could find her again, could I save her? If I saved her, what would happen to me?

I should not panic, I told myself. I would give myself time to think. I had time. If Sida had shown me anything, I thought, I had time.

But I was wrong, because Pa was back and trouble came at his heels.

CHAPTER EIGHTEEN

Business and Family

There was a covered cart outside the family hedge. After the first jolt of recognition, I realized it was different from the one Ma had at home, with its cunning wooden house perched on top of the wagon bed. This one had a frame covered by tanned leather and had bells bolted to the corners.

A muscular dun mare grazed in front of it, her forelegs hobbled to keep her from straying. Maro and Dan perched in a tree a few steps away, watching her with delight.

A horse?

I hadn't seen a horse in months. I had assumed that these people did not have horses. Now I knew that everyone around us was simply too poor to have them.

"What is it like, Lizbet?" Dan asked. He was the shyer of the two boys, so his words spoke to a special determination.

"What?"

Maro pointed "How do we…"

I realized that if there were seldom any horses around, my brush with Sida would be one of their only sightings of such animals. And Sida was much smaller than this work animal.

The mare looked up at us, her ears twitching. She knew she could not run and was made nervous by her vulnerability.

I put out my hand, palm down so she could smell it. "*Yimma naisik*," I murmured, using the same crooning tone Torun had used with Sida. I scratched her under the chin, stroked her cheek and her neck. She was so docile, so used to being touched.

"Come down from the tree quietly and slowly," I told the boys.

They came and joined me in patting the horse. "If you look in the cart, there might be brushes for her."

Dan went and came back with the stiff-toothed curry comb and the long-haired dandy brushes cradled in his arms. I showed them how to work the curry comb in circles over the horse's body, how it shook off loose dirt and old skin. She was tall for them, so Dan climbed on Maro's back to get at her shoulders.

"She should get brushed every day," I told them.

"That's what Pa said. He and Heino came back today, but Heino's in the village, selling."

"This is Pa's horse?"

Dan nodded, but they were deep in their task.

I left them and pushed through the hedge.

Melina and Sarai were cooking a stew over an open fire—as the weather warmed, we had started cooking outside. Although we usually ate on chairs made of stumps, today they had laid out a blanket a few feet away, on top of which lay a spread of leaven bread, candied ginger and chestnuts and ripe peaches. Pa sat on the blanket as well, playing slap-jacks with Telka. His hands lay lightly over hers and every few seconds she'd try to slap down on them, breaking into giggles each time.

When they saw me come in, Melina and Sarai regarded me with uneasy respect, as if I were somehow different and formidable. Telka flung herself at my legs. I gave her a kiss on the top of her head before she ran back to Pa. Being away from her for snatches of time made me see more clearly how she was growing. The baby-roundness of her face was slowly fading into Melina's delicately pointed chin. I felt a small twinge. For those who knew us well, she would not be my miniature as she grew, but Bettina's.

"Lizbet," my father said, his face split in a wide grin. "As promised, a share of the reward!" He sat Telka down on the blanket beside him and untied a small leather purse from his belt. He flung it to me and I caught it. It was heavy for its size. I teased open the drawstring and found the dull glint of gold and silver inside.

I couldn't help letting out a little gasp and my heart went tight. It was more money than I had ever seen. At home we didn't get so much for our medicine, and the money went into the coffer or was turned into meat and bread. With this much gold, a person could run away, set up a shop or a house or a herd. I took a few steps forward and held the purse out to Pa. Lording it over me, I thought. That would be just like him.

He shook his head.

"It's yours," Pa said. "I hope you don't mind that I spent a few coins on the horse and cart."

"No...no," I switched to Gersan, "of course not."

"They bought the horn and wanted more." He stood up and came to me. We were talking business, and he wanted it to be conducted in private. We strolled over to the lambing pens on the other side of the oak tree. "I said my lass could call the unicorns to her."

"They...they believed you?"

He put a hand to his chest and gave a neat bow. "I am known as an honest merchant of rare things."

My heart gave another squeeze. Why not? said a small voice in my head. Picking up a horn here or there...we could make a fortune. But then I remembered Julian and his fine clothes, the arquebus he brought hunting, though it was made for the battlefield. If he had no respect for me, who shared his blood, hunters like him would have no respect for the animals they hunted or the people who sought to protect them.

"You cannot sell any more horns whole!"

He frowned. I was ruining his fun. "Don't be absurd. They paid just to see the horn. Before I sold it, I made an obscene amount just letting people touch it! You should see their eyes light up, even as they part with their money."

"Fair enough, Pa. But I've been in this business longer and I know it. Ma sold ointment made from the alicorn. We lived well and helped many folk."

"I saw your face when you looked in that purse. You've never lived this well."

"We never told the secret of the unicorns. Like this...You'll attract the wrong kind of attention." I had to translate the danger to the unicorns into terms he would understand. "It was our medicine that gave us a reputation and kept us safe."

"Don't be a little idiot, Lizbet. For ointment, you need jars, grease...it costs time and material to produce. The horn doesn't need anything. I made twenty gold pieces for the whole thing and fifteen silver showing it off. A king's ransom. No."

"Hunters and kings won't let someone as lowly as you get the glory."

His body tensed up, his lower lip pushed out and his brow lowered. In Telka it would be laughable, but for a moment I was afraid he would hit me. Instead, he walked around in a circle, came back and gave the fencepost a great kick. The fence shuddered under my hands.

I stayed frozen where I was.

"You don't scare me," I said. Though I felt close to tears, I wasn't going to cower. I narrowed my eyes and looked over, ready to stare him down.

"Find me another horn, Lizbet." He was smiling again, careful and controlled.

I held out the purse to him again, though it was worth a future for a girl like me.

He shook his head. "Keep it. Think about it. Think about what you can get with money like that. It's summer now, an easy season. But summer will come to an end and times will be hard. This family does not suffer shirkers. You will have to help us as we have helped you. And as soon as you spend a coin in that purse, one coin, mind you, understand that we have a deal."

I felt a jag of fear in the bones of my arms, the muscles in my shoulders. At home, I had known what I had offered, but here, Pa was right. I didn't give anything much to the family and yet they had fed me and clothed me.

The next day proceeded normally—that is, I pretended it was normal for me to stay inside on a sunny day to help my sisters with their work.

Pa played along. He saw the purse tied at my waist. He knew that I was tempted despite myself. He whistled as he went out to tend the vegetable patch with the boys.

I wished that Torun were there, that I had time before the sun went down to go to him and ask him what was happening. But at the heels of that wish, I remembered Bettina and her tear-stained face. I didn't want to see him—how could I tell him about what I knew? Should I? Instead, I carded wool. I even worked a little on one of the small looms for making ribbons. I concentrated on making an even strip of red. Nothing fancy. I watched my sisters. They traded songs and rhymes, and my ribbon grew inch by inch.

"You're not horrible," Sarai told me. I almost blushed at the compliment, but she continued. "Still, you'd be better off in the forest getting more horns."

"I can't," I said. "It will bring hunters and rich men."

"I don't care," Sarai said. "That could be a good thing. I could sell my cloth to them."

"But you don't understand!"

"Don't I?" Sarai snapped. "Tell me, then!"

"He's offered me money if I can get more *uksarv* horns. But it feels wrong to sell my...my talent...when he's so greedy."

"What do you expect, Lizbet?" Sarai's voice was harsh. "Pa is never going to let us have any sort of freedom unless he gets his cut of the money first. Bettina understood that...why can't you?"

"Bettina gave us luck," Telka said into the silence, as she worked on her small handloom. "That's what Pa says. Sarai, if she didn't go to the Alvina, you wouldn't have gotten so good at weaving," Telka added with desperate certainty.

"Right," Sarai said, her voice torn between sarcasm and bitterness. She turned back to the loom and started weaving in a great clatter. In her anger, she counted her threads wrong, swore and started again.

Telka didn't have the spirit to fight back. She ducked her head and started to work quietly.

Between the sounds of their weaving, I listened to the little house in the trees creak and shift with the wind. Bettina had gone to the Alvina. What did that mean? When I saw her, she had looked angry and almost...almost wild. So, where was she? Where had she gone? The forest? But I had been there and hadn't seen a thing. I thought of the skull I had found years ago. Perhaps I wasn't looking in the right places.

But the thud of hooves interrupted my thoughts. I wouldn't have time to plan ahead.

CHAPTER NINETEEN

Old Magic

We piled out on the portico. I was worried that Sida had come to me, but Telka and even Sarai were excited by the possibility. Melina followed us so that she could round us up and send us inside.

Heino trotted in on a roan nag. I had a moment to wonder how much of my money had already been spent between the two of them and then Heino said something that sent the others into a panic.

"The old woman says it's her time," he shouted up to us. It took me a moment to remember Velni-Ani. My sisters' and brothers' grandmother who had called me *Alvinaisik*.

Melina gasped. She turned extremely pale, but the edges of her nostrils and the rims of her eyes were flushing pink. Heino dismounted and tossed his reins to Maro, as if he had been riding horses all his life. Or, more likely, as if he'd been an arrogant man all his life.

"They told me that you would host the supper, Melina. You're the next oldest in the family."

"When?" Melina said, her voice soft and flat.

"Tomorrow." There was a pause as Heino pushed through the hedge and climbed up to us. "I think I'll stay here tonight," he said. "No point in going back now."

Melina opened the door and rushed inside. We followed, leaving Pa and the boys to help Heino in.

As soon as Heino entered, I felt his eyes flick-flick-flicking from the loom to Sarai's discontented face to Melina's silent and swift movement from the hearth to the table. She picked up jars and dishes and put them down again, unsure what to do first.

I stood by the door without an idea of where to put my body. He saw me watching and winked.

Sarai rubbed at her right eye with the heel of her hand. "Does she have anything to wear?"

Heino shook his head. "She said you had shawls..." he trailed off. He and Pa exchanged glances. I imagined they considered these shawls as potential merchandise, not family possessions.

Melina nodded. She went to the alcove where her bed was, and pulled out the flat, rectangular box that lay underneath. This was where she kept her best pieces. She opened the lid and lifted out a neat stack of cloths. She pulled out one, two, three, four white shawls with long, trailing fringes. One of the shawls had a faint, reddish-brown smear on the edge, but Melina handled this one with the most care. Then she took out a shawl of joyous red with a fringe that was yellow like goldenrod.

"Do they have the food?" Melina asked.

"Yes. But she asked you to make honey cakes."

Melina's and Sarai's eyes met for a long moment.

"And she couldn't give us more warning?" Sarai said. Her voice was wet and angry enough for both herself and her mother.

"Is...is there a way I can help?" I said into the silence that followed.

Melina looked up at me with an expression that was close to hatred. Sarai put her hand over her mother's.

"Go make supper. Take Telka."

As I passed with Telka, Heino showed me his teeth. They were tiny, the milk teeth of a small child. Any child in Heino had died long ago. How could Pa be such a fool to bring him here? Telka's hand squeezed tighter around mine. Neither of us liked being near him.

Telka and I worked on the meal quietly. We fetched water and built up the fire next to the summer kitchen, a three-walled shed. I sent Telka with Maro and Dan to pick string beans, a few onions, and handfuls of dill and parsley. Then I chopped and fried the string beans and onions in mutton fat. Telka and the boys fed the fire and watched my progress hungrily, as they perched on seats made of sawed-down trunks. We ignored the muffled explosions of conversation in the house above us.

"Can we have dumplings, Lizbet?" Maro asked.

"The flour is in the house," I said. Then I remembered something. "Your Ma is making honey cakes. Ask if you can eat them."

The children exchanged uneasy glances.

Maro cleared his throat. "Those are for the Alvina," he said.

"I thought the Alvina were a story." I said.

Maro looked at Dan with his eyebrows raised. "Of course they're not!"

Dan tugged at one of his curls. "Maybe we can have eggs... I'll see if the hens laid any." He walked away and Telka trotted after him.

Maro was watching the sizzling onions and beans intently.

I cleared my throat. "At the village, they were mean to me. They thought I was an *Alvinaisik.*"

"People don't like the Alvina to come here. We go to them," Maro said. He picked up a stick and poked at the fire. Then he pushed the stick into the red, glowing heart of the flames and stood up. "I better get the fire in the oven ready if they're baking honey cakes." He walked away to the little brick oven on the other side of the summer kitchen. I was left to chop herbs and think. How was Velni-Ani going to meet the Alvina? How could Melina feel, knowing her mother was leaving her?

While I had made dinner with the younger children, Sarai and Melina had been busy at work with their own preparations. The next morning, all we had to do was obey their directions.

We set up a trestle table and rolled the trunk stools around it. We laid out a tablecloth and set onto it dishes filled with the treats Pa had bought in town, a platter of honey cakes, several links of smoked sausage and a set of thimble-sized cups, a tumbler, and a jug filled with fruit brandy. The boys scoured the grass for lingering sheep pats and took them to the midden heap in the back corner of the vegetable patch.

Having done all of this, we had nothing to do but change into our best clothes and wait. Melina lay down on her bed and drew the curtain. It took Sarai two deep breaths to go from satisfied with her work to anxious and bored. She took a handloom out onto the shady western side of the portico and told Telka and me to do the same. "No point in wasting time," she said as she started to work. Beside us, the boys carved spoons.

The air was still and humid. I felt the sweat prickle and form on my forehead, on the back of my knees.

I thought I heard my heart beating louder.

Tun-tun, tun-tun.

Telka turned her head to listen. No, it was not my heart. Sarai's hands slowed on her loom and she stood up from her stool. I followed her around to the section of the portico facing east towards the village.

Tun-tun, tun-tun. And now I could hear a low, steadily alternating whine.

The scrawny drummer and the old fiddler from the wedding emerged from the eastern forest. Behind them walked Rina and her mother supporting Velni-Ani between them. Lastly came a group of villagers headed by Rina's snub-nosed husband, Giron, all carrying baskets of food.

"Mama," Sarai called. "They're here."

She ran to the ladder and clambered down. Not knowing what to do, I watched from above.

Sarai tore across the yard, but as she reached the hedge, she paused to catch her breath. She disappeared through the bushes and emerged on the other side with her hair neat and her hands folded in front of her. The party of villagers met her and she bowed her head to them. The fiddler stopped to speak, but the drummer kept his rhythm. *Tun-tun, tun-tun.* Sarai nodded again and returned to the house. She climbed the ladder angrily, and it shook as she pulled herself up. I followed her to the door, but she didn't go into the house. Inside, Melina stood, frozen over the hearth. She had heard the drum; she had been waiting with folded shawls in her arms.

"It's time," Sarai said. "Maro, Dan, come. Telka, you stay inside. You're too young. Lizbet, look after her."

The boys climbed down the ladder and began greeting the villagers.

Telka's brow puckered. She went to her mother who stood in the doorway, but Melina simply shook her head and left us, one arm clutched around the bundle in her arms.

Telka tried again, turning to Sarai. "I want to go."

Sarai dug at her eye with her fingers. "No." Then she began climbing down.

Telka turned to me. "I don't want to go in. It's too hot."

I nodded. We crouched down and looked through the slats of the portico railing as Melina and Sarai showed the village men and women to the trestle table. They laid down their food and the warm air filled with the hum of conversation. The drum and fiddle ended their melody with a flourish.

The villagers formed a circle around Velni-Ani, and Sarai poured brandy into the small cups. Velni-Ani's tumbler was far larger than the rest, and she had to hold it in both hands to keep her wrists from trembling. After drinking deeply, she began a song in a wavering, broken voice and they all joined in. I couldn't understand the words and couldn't tell whether they were non-sense sounds or an older dialect.

After the song was done, they tossed back the drink and Sarai poured another round.

They sang and drank a second and a third time.

Velni-Ani nodded. She held out her hand and beckoned to Melina.

Melina held out the shawls, one by one, for the closest female kin. White for Rina. White for Rina's mother. White for Sarai and Melina. Joyous red for the grandmother. They folded themselves into the shawls, covering their hair. The tassels hung down to the hem of their skirts and trembled with each movement. After the women had adorned themselves and Sarai picked up the plate of honey cakes, the party made their way out of the family enclosure.

"Lift me up to see," Telka said. So, with Telka's milky breath on my cheek and her fat arms pressing into my neck, we watched.

The drummer took up his rhythm and the fiddler began to pull her bow across the strings. The women walked downhill, towards the river. Rina and Sarai held hands to make a seat for the old woman, and they carried her across the shallow water. Their shawl fringes trailed behind them, touching the water, flinging droplets upward with each step. On the other side, they put her down and the party kept walking along the path I knew so well.

"Are they going to the forest?" I asked suddenly.

"No, silly," Telka said, now wiggling to be set down. "They're going to the Alvina." I knelt and she released her arms from my neck. She sat down on the floor, then lay down to look up at the tree's canopy above us.

I had no idea of what to do, so I lay down beside her. I stared up at the overlapping green of the leaves. Patches of bright sky winked at us as the wind ran through the branches and disturbed the leaves. Then I turned my head to look at Telka. To my surprise, she was no longer staring up, but had her small hands over her eyes.

I rolled onto my stomach. "Telka, what is it? Are you all right?"

She pressed her hands closer to her face. "No! It's not fair. What...what if they see *her*? And I won't!" She lifted her hands from her face and slapped them down on the floorboards on either side of her. To my surprise, she was glaring at me. "Do you think they'll see her?"

Her...she must mean Bettina. "Telka, I don't know. I don't even know what your grandmother is doing all the way out here."

Telka pulled herself to her feet and walked over to where I sat. She threw her head back as if to see whether I was lying. "Don't you know?"

I shook my head.

"The Alvina live in a deep, deep cave and if you go there when you're old, you'll be young and live forever and be happy."

"So, your grandmother is going to stay with the Alvina?"

She nodded. "The Alvina gives the family good luck, too. If you go to them. It's old magic."

Magic. Torun had told me that there was no human magic. But here, Telka was telling me another story. I desperately wanted to follow them, to see what they saw.

I glanced at Telka. I couldn't leave her by herself. She'd have to come with me. She would probably follow me if I tried to leave her behind anyway. "Telka, you have to promise me you'll be very good and very quiet," I said.

"Oh, yes," she said. "I am very quiet."

I got my pack and we climbed down into the yard. As we passed the feast table, Telka deftly took two, thick-crusted meat and cheese pastries and rearranged the rest on the plate to make their absence invisible. Being the youngest of a large family, it seemed, was teaching her a certain slyness. She held them out to me and I put them in my pack.

I gave her a piggyback ride down and across the river and as we scrambled up the other side, I thought I saw a white glimmer to the southwest. Sida? This would be a bad, bad time for her to show herself, with all the villagers around. No, I heard drumming. It was Sarai, her tassels flying behind her as she ran. Her face was pinched with not crying.

Telka and I crouched down behind a boulder. I put my hand on the little purse full of silver and gold at my side so its clinking would not attract attention. We had missed whatever had happened. And now there was no way for us to go back inside without being seen.

Behind Sarai, the rest of the party walked slowly, singing a bittersweet tune as they picked their way across the river. The grandmother was not with them. A slight ribbon of rotten smell unwound from their path. They had come from the cave.

I waited until their singing faded into the trees.

"Let's go see the cave," Telka said. To stand, I put one hand in the scrub and was surprised to find the *uksarv* horn I had thrown away some days before. My fingers curled around it, and before Telka could see it, I put it into my pack. Tomorrow, I'd take it deep into the forest, where neither Pa nor Telka would find it.

Telka climbed onto my back and we set off toward Torun's boulder, with its leering, hungry mouth. Don't go south, he had said.

With hesitating steps, I passed the rock where I had met Torun, where I had frightened Bettina. I followed the path. At the fork I knew so well, I stopped and looked south. I breathed in deep and felt that tang of sulphur on the air. The air in my mouth tasted like rotting things. I ran from boulder to boulder, marking the leering faces. My heart began beating faster as I jogged a little further. There, on the right, another boulder, another face. Above me, the ravine was becoming rockier, more severe. I began to run. Telka's arms were tight around my shoulders. I turned the corner where the cliff jutted out. As I walked closer, the rock face receded. There I saw the scooped-out eyes, the bitten-off nose, the gaping mouth of the cave with its warm, fetid breath.

The air was thick in my lungs. I squinted into the cave's mouth, but saw nothing of Velni-Ani, not even a flash of a shawl fringe. You'll be young and live forever, Telka had said. They give the family good luck. A grandmother too weak to cross the river. One less mouth to feed. That was good luck to a struggling family.

Telka coughed, and I was struck with the monumental stupidity of coming here with her.

I backed away from the cave's mouth, away from the streaks of discoloured stone. I turned and stumbled to the foot of the clearing and then out of sight of the cave, where a slight breeze brought fresh air.

I put Telka down and she leaned her head against the shade-cool rock. I sat beside her and put my arm around her.

"Are you all right, Telka?"

She nodded, but her voice was shaky when she spoke. "We missed it," she said. "We didn't see anything." I took the meat pie from my bag and split it between us. Perhaps eating would make her feel better. It would give me time to think about what to say.

There is no human magic, Torun said. He had told me that he had once almost taken the path here, that he had once almost become lost. But Sarai and Melina spoke as if magic existed. I looked down the path towards the black maw of the cave.

Did they believe it? Sarai and Melina, Heino, Rina, Velni-Ani? And yet, why would you need to ceremonially drink a dizzying amount of brandy to cross over? Or did they just need a story to explain despair, exhaustion, hunger. No, the grandmother had gone knowingly to her death. But Bettina? Why had she chosen to do it, when she had her family, when she had her plans, when she had Torun to help her?

"Sarai will be so mad," Telka said after she finished eating. "I wasn't supposed to see. I was supposed to stay upstairs."

There was a sigh. Not mine. I looked up and saw Sida looking down at us. Her horn was the length of my hand now and she had filled out, growing broad in the chest and legs. She was beautiful and strong.

With big eyes, Telka held out her grubby hands to Sida. Sida smelled them and snuffled at Telka's hair. Telka laughed, forgetting her sorrow in a moment.

I was grateful for the distraction and got up. "Telka, this is Sida, my *uksarv*."

"I knew it," Telka said, following me.

Sida suffered herself to be petted for a bit and then trotted in front of us. She stopped in front of Torun's rock, where I had seen Bettina. And again, the stillness gathered in her muscles. We drew near.

"What's she doing?"

"Wait and see…"

I held my hand beside Sida, felt the moments build up beside her like a pile of feathers or layers of thinly stretched pastry dough. As I watched the moments blur around us, I knelt and picked up a stick and laid it through the gap.

For a flickering moment, we saw Bettina lounging on the boulder, leaning on her elbows and smiling with her face to the sun. She was at peace and happy. She was also younger than the last time I had seen her by some years. Her limbs were short-er, her curves were less pronounced, but to Telka it made no difference.

Bettina opened her eyes and looked straight at us. Her eyes widened. She sat up and smiled. Her smile was like the breath of spring. Like she knew the secrets of the world and they were worth knowing.

Sida shifted and stepped into another moment, the late summer day we had left.

My hand was still on the stick, and I felt the weight of the dense, thick layers of time. "That's…that's where she is?" Telka asked me. She put her hand in mine and squeezed my fingers.

"Yes," I said. "I think." She *was* there—in that moment, in the past.

"Good."

Sida looked at me with a long, considered glance. She had done this twice, twice shown me this place and Bettina in it. There was something about it that bothered her, I thought. Something that didn't fit. Something that had to do with Bettina, and with me.

Sida tossed up her chin and led us back north, closer to the place I crossed the river. I carried Telka across. When we reached the bank, I turned to check on Sida. She had disap-peared again. No matter, I thought. I had a way back.

"I'm hungry," Telka said.

"Go through the hedge on the other side," I said. "Say you were hiding behind the henhouse."

She giggled at this naughtiness and scampered off.

Telka's adventure was over, I thought, but not mine.

Perhaps I could find Bettina again.

CHAPTER TWENTY

Into the Woods

I ran back to the rock where we had seen Bettina but found that the stick I had left in the portal had snapped in half with the weight of time. I would have to find Sida again before I could get to Bettina.

I pushed myself up the switchbacks towards Fenlen Forest. When I reached the top of the ridge, I did not pause to give my blood. I did not think about the path I took, and my strides were certain. I sought to forget myself in action, but instead my thoughts crowded in on me. The evening air was cool against my face and I realized that summer would be turning into fall. Not soon, but it would inevitably come. Then winter, and with it, the anniversary of Bettina's disappearance. I wondered how they would commemorate it, whether there would be cups of brandy to fill and empty or songs to sing. Or if I could find her, as it seemed Sida wanted me to do...what then?

And perhaps because I had so completely forgotten my desire to go home, it happened.

I stumbled to a halt. That tree...It was a large birch that had been rubbed pink over successive generations of unicorns rubbing off their horn velvet. The hairs on my arms prickled. I knew I had found my old trail, that I had connected my two worlds. The tree was on the path I had been creating from Melina's house. Yet it was not far from Ma's clearing. I could walk home with my eyes nearly closed. Either home. The shock made my skin tingle as the world reoriented itself. I suddenly saw myself from two overlapping directions.

I was standing east, heading west. I could run back to Ma now. I could be there in two days. I would salve her bitterness with the knowledge that I had not abandoned her. I could have my routine of living my solitary life, grooming unicorns and jogging down the old paths on the hunt for alicorn. Or perhaps I would help my mother leave the log house and find a new life for herself elsewhere. One she had chosen.

I could walk away without finding out what had happened to Bettina. Without making sure that Telka got home without any trouble. Without saying goodbye to Torun.

I could go home, but not yet. I had work to do.

I turned back.

Retracing my steps, I made my way to where Torun and I had helped the doe deliver her fawn. The herd was on the move but couldn't have gone far. I saw the flattened circles of grass and whorls of disturbed loam where fawns had curled up and slept. I followed them north until I spotted Sida, her silver-grey coat standing out against the fading light. She was near the back of the herd, with the specked doe and her fawn.

They must have smelled the villagers at the base of the escarpment and decided it was unsafe to stay close to the edge.

The matriarch tried to nudge them into hurrying, but the fawn limped and was taking shallow, panting breaths. The doe gave a small kick, warning the matriarch not to push them. She led her fawn under the low-hanging branches of a pine tree and settled down there with her legs tucked under her. The fawn followed suit. When they lay still, they were almost invisible amongst the dead needles.

The matriarch paced worriedly in front of the pine tree. Sida came to her and mimicked her movements. The matriarch

stopped and Sida stopped as well. The matriarch stepped close
to her and leaned over to nip gently at Sida's mane, a sign of
recognition. She stepped aside and herded the rest of the
does and fawns away, leaving Sida to guard the speckled doe's
hiding place.

I let the herd retreat through the trees before I approached
Sida.

"I need your help," I said. "I need you to help get to Bettina."

Whether or not Sida understood my words, she understood
my tone, the anxious tang in my sweat, the tension in my shoulders. But she flared her nostrils and stepped backwards. She
wasn't going anywhere until the speckled doe and fawn were
ready.

"Well, I suppose I'm not going anywhere either." I sat down
by her feet and ate the cheese pie that was in my pack.

Underneath the tree, the fawn had fallen asleep. They
wouldn't be moving until daybreak. Unless I left for Melina's
house now, I realized, I would be here all night. If the family
hadn't realized I had snuck away, they would now. Or Telka
would have told. My stomach gave a swoop. What would they
think, to find me gone?

I kissed Sida on her broad cheek and hurried back to the
escarpment. I looked down over the valley. There was a bonfire
burning in front of the family enclosure and I could see the
black silhouette of people standing around it. The wind brought
snatches of song to me and the smell of woodsmoke.

But closer by, beneath me on the path, I saw a flicker of
something between the trees. Torchlight. Oh no. They had realized I was gone and had come looking for me. And then I saw
who it was. Heino, carrying a bundle with him in one arm and
a torch in the other. I gasped, and he looked up. His small teeth
glinted. I backtracked, but not quickly enough.

Heino caught sight of me and called out. "Holding out on us, are you? Well, I don't need you."

He dropped his bundle, which unfolded itself with a little whimper. Telka. Heino leaned over, seized one of her upper arms and pulled her up.

A surge of hate and fear weakened my knees as I remembered Julian looming over me all those years ago. I needed to save Telka, but in order to do so, I needed to be sly.

Heino took large strides for a man of his height. Telka stumbled forward. She couldn't see anything. The flame of the torch stopped her eyes from adjusting to the night.

I drew back into the shadows and heard a nicker. Stupidly, I had led them right to Sida.

I ducked down behind a tree. Heino moved his torch from right to left. He couldn't see me. I couldn't risk calling to Telka. Not yet. I slipped from tree to tree parallel to them as they walked forward.

A branch snapped under my feet and Heino chuckled. "I know you're there." They were too close to the speckled doe and her fawn. But Heino was blind to what lay outside his golden sphere of torchlight. He stepped right past the pine tree under which the doe was hidden.

A few more steps and he would pass by them completely. He would never know they were there. But he paused.

It was too close. Sida couldn't risk the danger to the doe and fawn. She stamped her feet in the darkness.

Heino turned away from the pine tree and took a few steps forward.

"Telka!" I shouted.

"It's you!" She stretched her short arms out towards me. "I'm coming!"

I snatched her up and ran out of the circle of torchlight. I crouched down under the pine with her. A grunt told me that the doe was there, awake, alert, but maintaining her stillness.

But Heino didn't care that Telka had disappeared. He saw what he had come for.

"Sida! Get back!" I called.

But Sida danced forward, stamping her hooves. Her horn was not long enough to look threatening, but long enough to be dangerous.

As she approached, Heino swiped in front of himself with the torch. The air filled with the smell of singed hair. Sida reared back with a shriek of fury. The skin on her right shoulder was red and raw.

"Come at me, you stupid beast."

She limped forward with her horn down.

In the dark, the cry of another *uksarv* cut through the still of the night. Not the matriarch, I thought. She wouldn't jeopardize the herd's safety.

The barrel-chested buck, the one who had stolen the speckled doe, had come to steal his prize away and now saw her threatened by a stranger. He stood beside Sida. His horn glinted dangerously in the torchlight. Though he was in danger, Heino's mouth twisted into a grin. I could see his thoughts clearly. The buck's horn was worth three times Sida's. The buck was the one he wanted.

Heino fumbled in his belt for a knife. It fell and he knelt to pick it up. That was his mistake. Sida and the buck charged at him. The torch went flying from his hand and rolled across the ground, setting alight the dry pine needles. I ran towards the torch and picked it up, stamping at the tiny flames on the ground with bare feet now thick-soled from my forest ramblings. Behind me, there was a scuffle as Heino started to run.

There was a scream and a thud.

Then the heavy breathing of the buck and Sida. And silence. I turned and raised the torch.

"Telka?"

"I'm here," she said, crawling out from under the tree.

She shook the branches as she came and a high bleat told me that she had woken up the fawn. Telka ran towards me and I hugged her to my side.

At the sound of the fawn, Sida and the buck emerged from the shadows. They were equals in strength and in their determination to protect.

Telka gasped at the sight of them. The buck bobbed his head at her, but he did not seem to think she was dangerous. Instead, he ducked his head under the branches to look at the fawn, who emerged looking a little sleepy, but fresh and alert. The doe followed her fawn and guided it in the direction the herd had gone. The buck turned back to Sida, who was limping. He touched his horn against her burned shoulder, place by place. She stood patiently while he worked.

Watching, I realized the horn's healing power had to do with time. It turned a fresh wound into an old one, encouraging scabs to form more quickly to protect the flesh from the world.

After a few minutes, the buck stepped away. The four of them moved close together and then walked off into the night, following the herd.

I wanted to call Sida to me, but I had Telka to look after. She was shivering with exhaustion, wonder and fright.

"Do you think you can climb on my back?" I said. I had the torch in one hand—I wouldn't be able to hold her with both arms. She shook her head. I sat down on the cold earth with her and she curled into me.

I wished I could put out the torch. My arm was aching and it was making me see spots of light in the darkness. No.

There were more torches. More people. My gut clenched. More hunters?

"Heino!" It was Pa's voice. "Where's my little girl?"

"Pa!" I cried. "We're here!"

I tried to rouse Telka and she groggily stood. I picked her up and we walked slowly through the dark towards the light.

They had stopped.

I saw Pa kneeling beside Heino and turned Telka's face towards me. Behind Pa were Giron, the drummer, and a few others. They watched us suspiciously.

At first, I did not see the wounds. And then, the red, damp holes, two of them, a thumb's width wide, right where his heart lay.

Pa sat down on a fallen tree. "I don't think the unicorn hunting would be a profitable plan," he said quietly.

"No." I swallowed. This was his way of admitting that I was right. The night's events had made the spit thick in my throat. "Do we take the body?" Telka shivered in my arms and then went very still.

Pa looked at Heino and then quickly away. "I don't think it's ours to take."

I took a step closer and saw why he had so spoken. The forest had already begun to claim the corpse. Vines had furled around his arms, between his fingers. Grass already poked through the weave of his shirt. Buds and leaves spread through his hair. I was reminded that I had never been at home in the Fenlen Forest. I had only ever been a guest. For the first time, I fully felt the honour of rambling through the trees in utter safety.

"Give me my child." Pa took Telka very gently, without looking into my eyes. He held out the torch and we began walking back. The darkness was starting to break; the sky was no longer black, but a deep blue against the trees. I recognized the path even in the murk. Guest I may be, but the forest had begun to be familiar again.

My heart hurt. Sida had not waited for me. Perhaps she had outgrown me. A thought occurred to me suddenly: would Ma welcome me home if I no longer had the unicorns? She must, I thought. She must.

Moaning in her sleep, Telka nestled closer in Pa's arms and he stroked her hair. "I told you not to run away in the night," he said to me.

"Look who's talking," I shot back. But my tone was half-hearted. I knew he was thinking about Bettina's disappearance. The other men muttered behind us, not daring to stray too far from us.

Pa's brow wrinkled and he shifted Telka in his arms. "I never knew what a miracle it was that I made it across," he said suddenly. "That night, when I left."

"Why *did* you leave? You and Ma were a mismatch, I understand that. But why leave then? Why there?"

"I botched it. We had sold bad stock all down the road. The trick of selling cheap pots and pans at high prices to poor folk is to keep moving. Never go back until they forget their anger. But the road ended. I might have been lynched."

"Over a cracked pan?"

"I might have also passed on bad coins. And I cuckolded a man three villages before."

"Pa!"

He shrugged. "Sylvia found out about it all, of course. She was giving me freezing hell. You'd know how it is, of course. Cold looks, sharp words and elbows."

"You deserved it."

"Ah, did I? I was a few years older than you. Torun's age."

I coughed in surprise. I could not imagine Pa near my age,

with a small child, a wife. It was like imagining that Telka was my child or that Torun had left her alone at a forest's edge. Impossible. We were out of the forest now, at the switchbacks. I went first and then held my arms out to make sure that Pa kept his balance.

"I was scared out of my mind," he said. "So I took the pony and rode away. As I went through the forest, the trees loomed and there were strange animal sounds. The pony threw me and ran away with the money. I had nothing. And I prayed that I would change my ways, that I would start again."

"Of course," I said, but he didn't catch my sarcasm.

Pa wobbled on a loose stone, and I steadied him. I did not want him to drop Telka.

"I have done honest trade, though I drive a hard bargain and keep my eye sharp for a good chance. I have kept faith with Melina. And I do not want to lose any more children." This last part he said rather fiercely, as if I should forget that he had already lost Bettina, that his deal with Heino had almost lost him Telka.

"You know," he continued, "sometimes I think I should have let Bettina come trade with me." Pa gave a wet sniff. If he cried, he'd scare Telka, so I patted him on the back. We walked together in silence. This was the first time I had talked to my father as an adult. I still did not like him, neither did I trust him. Tomorrow, he'd be preening and self-contented. But in this moment, I let myself feel sad for him, just a little bit.

CHAPTER TWENTY-ONE

Alvinaisik

When we got back, the bonfire had burned low. Two dark shapes stood out against the glow. Melina and Sarai. Melina stood there, in front of it, with her shoulders hunched. When the group of us reached her, she strode over to Pa and took Telka from him. She nodded to the men. "Please, go upstairs and sleep. I thank you for your efforts."

"And the *Alvinaisik*?" That was the drummer.

Sarai looked at me swiftly, and I realized that Melina had not yet acknowledged me.

"Lizbet has done nothing wro...." Pa began, but Giron cut him off.

"Nothing? She stole the child."

"Heino stole her," Pa shot back

Melina gave Telka to Sarai. "Take her up to sleep."

Telka mumbled something and then burrowed her face into Sarai's neck.

Sarai's grim face contorted, as if she were about to say something, but then she just nodded and retreated.

Sarai and Telka knew me and liked me. Now they were gone. Torun was up in the high pasture. And the men did not trust my Pa.

"Heino stole her," Pa repeated. "Lizbet brought her to me."

"But who took the child to the *Alvina birlan*?" Giron said. "Why is Heino dead?"

"Because he was a fool," Pa said. "Like the lot of you."

"You're the fool," Melina cut in. "Charmed by an *Alvinaisik* when your daughter is gone. Bettina left us, and you expect me to accept *her* instead?"

"I am my own self," I said, but my voice was faint. I swallowed and raised my voice. "I am not an *Alvinaisik*. I passed your tests. I walked across poppy seeds. I wear iron. I learned to weave. You judge me by rules that I don't know. But I am not a *hekunaisik* that you can throw your sadness on."

Melina waved her hands, dispelling traditions like so much smoke. "I did not want to believe it. But Bettina said she had a creature haunting her. She disappears, and you appear. You enchant Torun and Telka. My mother did not trust you and suddenly she decides to join the Alvina. You are a danger to us."

One of the men gave out a low growl and I became horribly aware of the fire next to us. Would they shove me in it and watch me burn? The river was too low to drown me in…

"Tomorrow, I will watch you go back to your home." Melina said firmly. "To the *Alvina birlan*."

Pa began to speak, but Melina raised her hand again. "You go with her or you stay with me."

He looked at her, the men and then me. He had known them for far longer than he had known me. I gave a small shrug and he stepped to Melina's side.

They locked me in the henhouse. For a mad moment, I thought they would light the entire building on fire. But the presence of the chickens reminded me that they would not waste food.

The hens clucked unhappily as I crouched among the straw and the sharp, ammoniac smell of their droppings. Telka and the boys liked poking around in here, but it was cramped for a grown person. I still had my pack, but it was too dark to find the knife I would need to flip the lock. I fumbled in a panic.

There was a soft scraping, the sound of a log being taken away from the door.

Was it already time? How?

The door opened and Sarai's slim form stood behind it.

"I brought your boots," she said. "And your coat."

I began to crawl out of the henhouse and when I was half out, Sarai pulled me the rest of the way. She brushed me off with short, hard motions.

"Thank you." I said as I pulled on my boots and my coat. "How did…"

"I came back outside to listen," she said. "You were an idiot to take Telka out there on a day like this. But they are fools, too."

I gave her a brief hug and let go. "Will you be all right?"

"Why shouldn't I?" She gave me a small shove. "Now go away. While you have time. Please." After closing up the henhouse, Sarai climbed the ladder to the house without looking back.

I slipped through the hedge quickly. With no one to see us, my escape really would seem like magic.

I could have crossed the river then, but I couldn't walk away into the night. Not just yet.

The men had thrust their torches into the fire, which was burning down slowly. I took one of them and set out in the direction of the high pasture. But I didn't go far. Just out of earshot and out of the line of sight from the house, at the lip of the trees, I spotted a small, low fire. As I went closer, I noticed sheep huddled and sleeping. One of Torun's dogs jogged through the whispering grass and smelled my hand before disappearing again into the night. Torun stood by the low flames.

"Did you find them?" he called. He had seen my light but had not yet recognized me.

"Telka's safe," I said, coming near and setting my torch into his fire. "She's sleeping upstairs."

Hearing my voice, Torun ran towards me.

"Elizabeth!" he said. He opened his arms and I stepped into

his embrace. "They said you left…" he said into my hair. It was the first time he had used my proper name and I leaned into him. "I thought you were gone." We sat down near the fire on his big shepherd's coat. Torun settled heavily into my side and he wrapped the ends of the coat around us like a blanket.

"I came back for sheep shearing, but…" He trailed off.

But he had arrived in time for a funeral feast for a woman gone to the Alvina. He had arrived in time for me to go missing. He had come home to his own personal nightmare.

I told him about what had happen in backwards order. About Sida's attack. Heino following me with Telka. Telka and Sida.

He interrupted me before I could mention whom Telka and I had seen with Sida. "Maro told me you had disappeared. And then Telka…"

A strange anger filled me.

"Why didn't you come with them to find me?" Pa had failed me, but I expected more from Torun.

"They would not let me come. They don't trust me to help them carry out their superstitions. They don't trust me around you…" He trailed off.

I thought of Melina's accusations. *You enchant Torun*, she had said. "It's like I'm the *hekunaisik*," I said.

Torun nodded. "When Bettina disappeared, no one knew why. You are the other girl. They can put their fear and their anger on you."

"And what do *you* put on this other girl?"

He nudged a stick further into the fire. "You wanted me. Like I wanted you. Like I wanted Bettina." He glanced away, ashamed, but I caught his face in my hands and looked at him. She had been his friend, Torun had said. They had planned to be married, but that was Bettina's childish way of imagining escape. In the end, she had left him behind. While I…I ran up to the high pasture to see him. I teased him and claimed him as my own.

I tried to keep my voice calm. "Then am I an *Alvinaisik* to you?"

"No. You are not like her." His voice was rough. "You are your own self."

That was not enough to make me stay. Still cupping his face, I kissed him gently. "I found my old path. The one that could lead me home."

"I'll come with you," he said.

It was a brave thing to say, but I did not believe Torun would abandon the herd which was his livelihood or the family who gave his life meaning. And I had not told him everything.

"Don't choose yet," I said. "Listen, Torun, I went to the Alvina's cave. And..."

"And?" To my surprise, Torun did not look angry or skeptical. The look in his eyes was scared, pleading. "Did you see anything?"

"I don't know." I had no more words because the hope in his voice broke my heart. We sat side by side, watching the fire. "I've been thinking about it since we saw the *uksarv* disappear. And since I learned about the *hekunaisik*." I cleared my throat. "I have a story for you, Torun. Plants and animals are born from the Life Tree, they spend a time above Earth Mother, warmed by their Sun Father and then return to her belly to sleep, only to be born again soon. One spring is like the next and if this winter is particularly harsh, in a hundred winters from now there will be another just like it. And to Earth Mother those winter days and summer nights are the same. The unicorns know this, and so they can pass between moments that are years apart.

"But humans left the forest and forgot Earth Mother. They started to count the cycles of the seasons and call them years and to use years to count lives and deaths. And now we don't live like the animals and the plants. I won't be born again into this world because I am Elizabeth and not anyone else, and you are Torun and not anyone else. But what if that's not quite right? Because to the forest, at least, I'm not Elizabeth and you're not Torun. We're just bits of earth and heat that can be put together and taken apart and put together again in time."

There was a pause. Torun said slowly. "I hear your story, but I do not catch the meaning."

"Here's what I think. I grew up in the forest and I have learned that time works differently there. And I can use that knowledge." I took his hands from around my waist and he curled them in his lap. "Torun, if…if you could know that Bettina was alive and safe, what would you give?"

He pulled away from me a little. "How can you ask that? I knew her all my life. She was my friend and now she is gone. I would give anything."

We stared at each other.

I wanted him to hold me to his side and tell me never to leave. Or I wanted to throw something at him, push him, scream. But clinging to him or hurting him would not give me what I needed, I realized. My desperation would not exempt me from my choice.

I had to save her and I couldn't stay here.

I stood up. I would have to go now, before anyone woke, before anyone could follow me. I didn't know what would happen. I opened my pack and fumbled through it, then placed the *uksarv* horn and the little jar of alicorn ointment I had onto the grass. The family could make use of them as they saw fit. "My village's name is written on here," I said, showing the label. "Maybe you can find someone to help you find it. If…If you ever needed more of it."

"I will find you," he said.

"Thank you."

Dawn was breaking now and I left my torch to burn in the fireplace. I wouldn't need it where I was going.

CHAPTER TWENTY-TWO

Found, Lost

I went back to the place where Sida had opened time, where my snapped stick lay. I looked at the thin, dry length of wood. It wasn't very strong, after all. Or else...I couldn't quite see its ragged edges. I put my hand to the stick and drew it through the air. At first, I felt nothing. I tried again, and...there. That slight tickle under the nail of my smallest finger. Sida left the edges of time messy, unsealed. If I put my other hand...there...I could feel the soft rips, like the pages of a book thumbed into softness. Did *uksarv* leave certain places open, or was Sida merely young and careless?

I searched for the first sting of winter's cold and drew my hand back. I let the filmy days of late autumn fall past until I saw a thin layer of snow covering the ground. A fresh set of footprints led from the boulder to the cave.

She had gone then.

I stepped through into the cold day and ran. The heat of the cave melted the snow into red mud.

Bettina was at the lip of the cave. She had her back to the warm stone and her arms were crossed. Her eyes were closed. She was steeling herself to turn and walk inside.

"Stop!" I shouted.

Her eyes fluttered open and she saw me.

I grabbed her by the shoulders and flung her away from the cave's edge. She tried to bolt past me, but I caught her by the arm.

Bettina pushed me away, then pulled at her clothing for anything that might protect her from me. She wouldn't have any iron on her, I knew she would be thinking. As a last resort, she balled her fists and squared her stance. There were no rocks small enough to throw here.

I stepped towards her.

She pushed me and I grabbed onto her wrists as I fell back. We hit the ground, with her on top of me. She twisted one of her hands away and swung her fist at my face.

When my nose broke, the metallic tang of my blood ran down over my top lip.

I let go of her other arm in surprise. She stood up shakily, clothing askew, and turned back to the mouth of the cave.

"Stop!" I cried out in Gersan. I was so flustered I lost my other language. "I don't want to fight you!"

The sound of my true voice made Bettina pause. She turned.

We stared at each other and a small smile twisted on her lips. My lips. Pa's lips.

"You strange creature," she said. As I remembered, her Gersan was good, much better than my Verian.

I wiped my bloody nose with the back of my hand. The throbbing pain made it hard to think. "Bettina, don't go into the cave."

She laughed, but it was not the joyful sound I remembered from my childhood. "Why not? At first, I thought I was being haunted by myself. But last winter, when you came to me in Telka's shape..."

"No! That was years ago for me!" How could her memory be so different from mine? "I was scared, and you were kind to me."

"But that was a mistake. I should have known when you threatened to follow me home."

"I wasn't...Bettina, I was lonely."

"I do not blame you," she said. "After all, how could you know how humans feel?"

"I *am* human. You know I didn't follow you home. Like I told you then, I went back to my own mother. I lived with her for years and years!"

"But then why did I keep seeing you? And why did you grow to match my size so quickly?"

"What do you mean?"

"Don't pretend to be innocent. You've been haunting me."

"What?" I remembered what Melina had accused me of, but I had no such memories.

"I heard you singing in the forest some days when I went foraging." She laughed through her tears. "But I've heard you warn me. Your voice in the woods." And she sang: *Blow away the dust, good wind, blow away the dust. With my heart's old sorrow, take it to the dusk.*

"How?" I had not seen *her*, though I had been close to the unicorn herd while I sang. She had been gone. I had come after. Unless...

"And I saw you with Torun. The first time I tried to run away, I saw you with him, standing in the river, naked."

"We...that wasn't..." Sida's grasp on time must have been shaky after the stress of the fawn's birth, but I could not explain that to Bettina. I remembered hearing what I thought was a night bird's cry. It must have been Bettina's shocked exclamation.

She waved me off. "No, the pathetic thing was how happy you looked that night. For me to be happy like that, I would have to be another person altogether. So, I might as well let the *Alvinaisik* have my place. And if you come from out here, then there must be a better place for me wherever you come from." She gestured at the cave and gave a little, skeptical wheeze of a chuckle. "But why would *you* leave? Why come *here*?"

I took a deep breath. "I came here to save you." If I couldn't convince her I was human, I might as well use her belief that I was *Alvinaisik*.

She laughed again, a real laugh this time. "Don't lie. Not to me."

"Don't walk into the cave. You'll die there. And if you cross the forest, if you survive, you won't find some better world, just another world with other problems." I racked my mind for ideas. "Torun said that you had a plan, that the two of you…"

"Torun won't leave," she said with disgust. "He's a shepherd. He takes care of sheep and people and that's all."

It sounded like a great deal to me, but I kept quiet. I thought of Ma, of her bitterness. Ma felt, somehow, like she had always chosen wrong, like she was living the wrong life. Although she couldn't live under Victor's thumb, she still thought she had been wrong to run away. Then, after Victor visited us the first time, she had been determined to set us apart. Even though we lived near the Helders' village, we would never be part of the community.

"*This* is not enough for me," Bettina said vehemently, spreading her arms. "The village is so…so *small*. Pa won't take me anywhere because I'm more valuable at home. And stupid Torun doesn't see a chance when it's right in front of his nose. I told him to run off and send for me. Instead, he bought me a lamb. He told me we could grow a flock. It was sweet, and I hate him for it." She kicked at the ground.

I thought of Pa's need to wander. When he felt trapped, he had abandoned us and now he arranged his life to make himself the most free. But he never extended that liberty to anyone else. Bettina was as much his daughter as Sarai and Telka and I were. "So, you want to walk into that cave? You'd rather end your life than try to survive the one you have?"

"I don't have a choice. I am losing the person I once was and the person they want me to be. Either I walk away or I hate everything and everyone around me." The anger drained from her. "I don't want to do that. They don't deserve it. They're not bad. I am. At least this way they'll get to keep their idea of me."

She had judged correctly, and I had suffered for it. "That's not fair, either," I said.

"Life isn't fair."

I almost smiled because I now knew where Sarai had gotten her toughness from.

I thought of what Torun had once said to me. "What if you just walked away?" I swallowed. "What if they didn't own you? Everyone thinks you're dead. You...you just disappeared. Just," I couldn't believe what I was saying. "Just walk away. Go to the cities. Sell your trade."

"Walk away with what?" Standing there in her shift and skirt, with her woven belt and white shawl, she was just a peasant girl, barefoot in the wild and the cold. "I have nothing. Anyone who knows Pa will send me home. Don't think I haven't tried before."

"You have to get past the village and then buy a horse." I fumbled at my belt, where I had tied the small purse of money Pa gave me. "Take this." I shrugged off my pack and tossed it at her feet, then pulled off my boots and threw them to her, one by one. "And these."

Bettina picked through my things. "The money won't disappear?"

I shook my head. "It's enough to set up shop." She might as well have the money.

"Hmph." She tugged on my boots. I gave her my coat as well and she dropped the shawl on the ground, where the red ochre seeped into the white fabric. They would find it the next day, I realized, and draw their own conclusions.

As she dressed, she looked more like me and less like Bettina. In my boots and coat, her suspiciousness made her look hardened and ready to walk for days.

She caught my eye and stared at me uneasily for a moment. I was wearing her skirt and shift and belt. "It's so uncanny. Like my own idea of myself." She stepped close to consider me. "And you've been haunting them?"

I nodded, succumbing to the story she would understand best. "But not anymore. A haunting is only useful when the wound is fresh and deep. I'll be gone in a year," I said. "It'll be safe for you to come home then."

"What if I don't want to come home in a year?" Bettina said, suspiciously.

"Then don't."

"Then maybe I will."

"Do as you please."

Bettina laughed at that and I saw an echo of her in happier days. She turned and set off, shoulders squared. It would snow sometime in the night and cover her tracks.

She was going to seek her fortune.

Now I would have to find mine.

I turned and slowly made my way to the portal. My nose ached and I almost regretted giving Torun the alicorn ointment. I fumbled my way through to early autumn, walking to spite my sadness. Though I moved slowly, time raced through the dawn, through the forest-green day and into the evening.

I stopped when the path was too dark to see and I lay down on the moss. I looked into the canopy and the sky beyond it as the stars began to emerge from the darkness. The cool night's air began to chill my sweat-soaked clothing. I could catch a cold, I mused. Perhaps I would die out here in the forest and no one would ever find me, like Julian. Ma wouldn't know that I hadn't abandoned her, not on purpose. I had probably broken little Telka's heart again. And Torun? I didn't know what I felt. Something snorted in the dark, as if to mock my self-pity. I didn't bother to look over until I saw Sida's face staring down at me.

"Hello, baby." She had become so big, I realized. Her face had elongated, her chest was well muscled and her mane was longer. She had not been a baby for a long time. "What have you been up to, you rogue?" I said.

Sida snorted again and touched my nose with her horn. As the pain eased and the swelling decreased, I looked at her. The burn on her shoulder was fully healed now, a rippled strip of dark grey scar tissue partially covered by her thicker winter coat.

I hadn't even gotten out at the right time, I realized. It had been late summer when I left and I was in autumn. A day had passed for me, but Torun and Telka and Sarai and the boys wouldn't have seen me for a month, at least. I had not left any tracks or traces to follow.

I touched my nose. Under the crust of dried blood, I knew my face would always look a little off balance. My nose would be a mark of my experiences and this certainty gave me strange comfort. I rolled over and stood up slowly. My muscles ached from exertion and cold.

Sida stamped her hooves.

"I know," I told her. "I'm the rogue." I reached out to run my hand along her body. The ache faded from the chilled joints in my fingers. Sida stepped forward, slowly enough that I could move with her. I stepped, and then she went forward again.

"Where's your herd, Sida?" I asked.

She gave a grunt.

Perhaps she had moved on, perhaps she had chosen me over them. Or perhaps I wasn't watching properly.

From the corner of my eye, I could see little flickers of gold, like moonlight falling through the gaps of leaves. A hoof here, a snatch of mane there. A curved horn. They were taking me home. She had grown up and moved on.

"You want to walk now?"

She did, and I followed until I began stumbling. Every once in a while, I snuffled a little into her coat and she suffered my occasional self-deprecating moans in patient silence. Had I chosen correctly? There was no right choice. But what if…I was mired in the circularity of these thoughts except when Sida gave me irritated nudges.

We came to my old home, the old familiar clearing, where an old, pale sliver of moon barely illuminated the shallow creek and the long meadow grass. Sida walked me to the edge of the forest. There was the pony cart, but there was no vegetable patch, no small house, no mule or dogs. Just the sound of a small child trying to be brave.

We had arrived at the beginning of things.

Sida stepped forward into the past, where in a few moments I would run out and see her. I stayed in the undergrowth, unsure whether I wanted to watch.

When the door to the pony cart opened, I looked away and found the old matriarch of Sida's herd watching me. I reached forward and she put her velvet nose into my palm. I closed my eyes and felt the fluttering of moments rush by me. Branches and leaves flickered in and out of life around my body, licking my hand and arms and legs before dying away again. When I opened my eyes, the matriarch was gone and I saw my mother's house and garden patch in the clearing.

I tramped heavily to my mother's door. But the house was locked and there was no fire on the hearth to cast a cheery light through the cracks in the shutters. There were dead leaves on the doorstep. The pony cart was gone as well. Had she left for good? I threw my weight against the door. The wooden latch broke and in the fading light I saw bare shelves, an empty floor.

Where was she?

The Helders were the only people I could think of asking, so

I began my trek to the village. It was dark when I arrived and the houses all looked strange and squat on the earth and bare without so many trees to shield them. I went right to Mrs. Helder's back door. I needed someone to cry with, someone large, old and jolly, who would give me bread with butter.

I knocked once, twice, three times.

And Ma opened the door.

CHAPTER TWENTY-THREE

Until a Few Days Ago

I live alone now and the seasons have changed twice. Poor Mrs. Helder died soon after I was lost and Ma dropped by to make Nicholas some consolatory stew and mingle her grief with his. Part of me believes that my disappearance helped her let go of her nobility and her isolation. A smaller, meaner part thinks she was waiting to be the only woman of the house, but she and Nicholas are happy together so I hold my tongue and watch. I see my mother with different eyes, how age and hard weather have made her majestic.

Once a week, Ma and Nicholas Helder come and fetch me to the village, where I give them what alicorn I have found for books and ink and strings of sausage. It is like we are ever repeating my return, with me falling into her arms and her stroking my hair with her muscular hands. The scene gives us both comfort. She does not mind that I find less alicorn because she says that rarity is good for business. She has invited me to come live in the village, but I am tired of fending off the proposals of the innkeeper's son and the master potter. I have become, it seems, a businesswoman and an heiress to a modest fortune of herbal ointments.

When I came home, I started taking over the family trade. I told Ma that I needed to know more of the world and that I could tell a better story about our products anyway. I say they're plant based and I've added things like rosehip jellies and raspberry teas to our selection.

I have the unicorns, but they do not come often. I begin to wonder whether I see fewer unicorns now because I am somehow tainted by the world. Or perhaps it's that, what with visiting Ma and our trips, my walks have been short and I have stayed too close to the edge of the forest. In the fall, Sida brought me her twin fawns. She let me run my hands along the curves of their necks, the dip of their backs. I fed them sugar and cinnamon, but they didn't stay for long.

A few weeks ago, during my spring trip, I was selling alicorn ointment at a fair in a city to the south when I saw a fine woman ride by in a gown of indigo. The hem had a thick border of white peacocks in a geometric style. The threads were of silk, not wool, but I squinted at her and recognized the curl of her dark hair under her fashionable hat and veil.

I slid out of the booth that Ma and I had set up.

"Bettina!" I cried, pushing through the crowds to get to her. "Bettina, *ti vog?*" She reined in her horse and looked down, startled.

I saw that she was far older than she should be, in her thirties at least.

"*Alvinaisik,*" she said. "Time has played tricks on us both, I see."

"You are well?"

Her smile was controlled. "As well as any master weaver. Apprentices are not what they used to be. I don't live here, you know," she added, wrinkling her nose as if she was used to something much finer. "But there's a dye merchant who has some stock I'm interested in."

"Did you ever go back?"

She was evasive. "Sarai and Telka work with me, but the boys are in the village with my parents." It was a way of telling me that I was not invited into her home or her private life. She paused, as if unsure whether to say more. "The homestead's been abandoned these past ten years. They say it's haunted. People still tell stories about you, you know."

"About me? I was only there for a few months."

Her smile became firm, hostile. "Don't play innocent, *Alvinaisik*. You haunted the family and stole a young man away. He walked away into the forest and was never seen again."

"Why would Torun do that?"

"To have you of all creatures ask such a question!" Bettina pressed her spurs to her horse and rode away quickly, without a backwards glance. I was left in the busy fairground with my heart like a clenched fist.

When I came home, I looked around at my quiet house, at my orderly garden. I have let my world become too contained. I have forgotten how truly strange life can be, and to remind myself, I have set to writing down my thoughts.

When I have finished this page, I will set it aside in my drawer, alongside my best recipes. I will pack up my things, with enough food for a few days. I will pull on my new boots, shoulder my bag and lock the door behind me.

The forest has many secrets, and I hope there is at least one more waiting for me.

Glossary of Verian Words

In writing of my experiences, I have translated some of the
Verian into Gersan—as I understood more of the language, it
become more transparent to my understanding. But there are
some words which I did not translate, for they seemed to hold a
certain pungent flavour of their own.

Birlan	cave	*Ufoli*	foreign
Bivin	wild	*Uksarv*	unicorn
Gorongos	frog	*Utta*	ewe
Heirre	come here	*Voon*	lamb
Hekunaisik	wooden girl	*Vog/vogmi*	are/am
Hin-ye	we're here	*Yimma*	good
Kesilik	get ready	*Zafor*	rain
Ki-yen	who's there	*Zasto*	bad
Kurre	out	*Zastola*	terrible
Naisik	girl		
Ni	no/not		
Sheled	brat?		
	(I never figured this word out entirely.)		

I do also have a phrasebook, which I began a few months after
coming home. I realized that certain words were slipping from
my memory, so I wrote them down. It should be somewhere
in the drawer, in the book whose first few pages are filled with
recipes. Though now that I think on it, I'd best take it with me.
—E.M.

ACKNOWLEDGMENTS

Thank you to Amy Tompkins at Transatlantic Literary Agency and Catharina de Bakker and Mel Marginet at Yellow Dog. I am grateful for their excellent questions, enduring generosity and cheerful support.

Thank you to Melissa Walter for reading the first version, before it morphed from short story to novel, while Maria Robson, Arden Hegele, Joanne Leow, Deirdre Baker, Christine Choi, Joanna Krongold, Emese Hegedus and Kati Tausz were great listeners during the process. Christa Jeney, Tom and Nora Magyarody were there before the beginning.

Thank you to the many parts of my family, who helped me learn about folk customs like the *kiszebáb* (and see them enacted in Cleveland), enjoy the power of communal song, bother the weavers at Szentendre, go to Estdocs to see that documentary about *rahvariietus* and mangle my Tatar vocabulary in Orenburg.

Thank you to Iliya Sigal for reading many drafts, and to Aaron for arriving right on time.